MIDNIGHT ECHO

Issue 17 — August 2022
www.australasianhorror.wordpress.com/midnight-echo/

I0584531

Like us on Facebook
Follow us on Twitter

Produced in Australia

AHWA

ACKNOWLEDGEMENTS

Production Team:

Guest Editor
Greg Chapman

Cover Art
Shane K Ryan

Layout
Greg Chapman

Proofreaders
Matt Tighe
Paul Sheldon

The Staff Would Like to Thank

Midnight Echo's fantastic contributors, readers, and fans.

CONTENTS

††AHWA Short Story Competition Winner 2021

†††AHWA Flash Fiction Competition Winner 2021

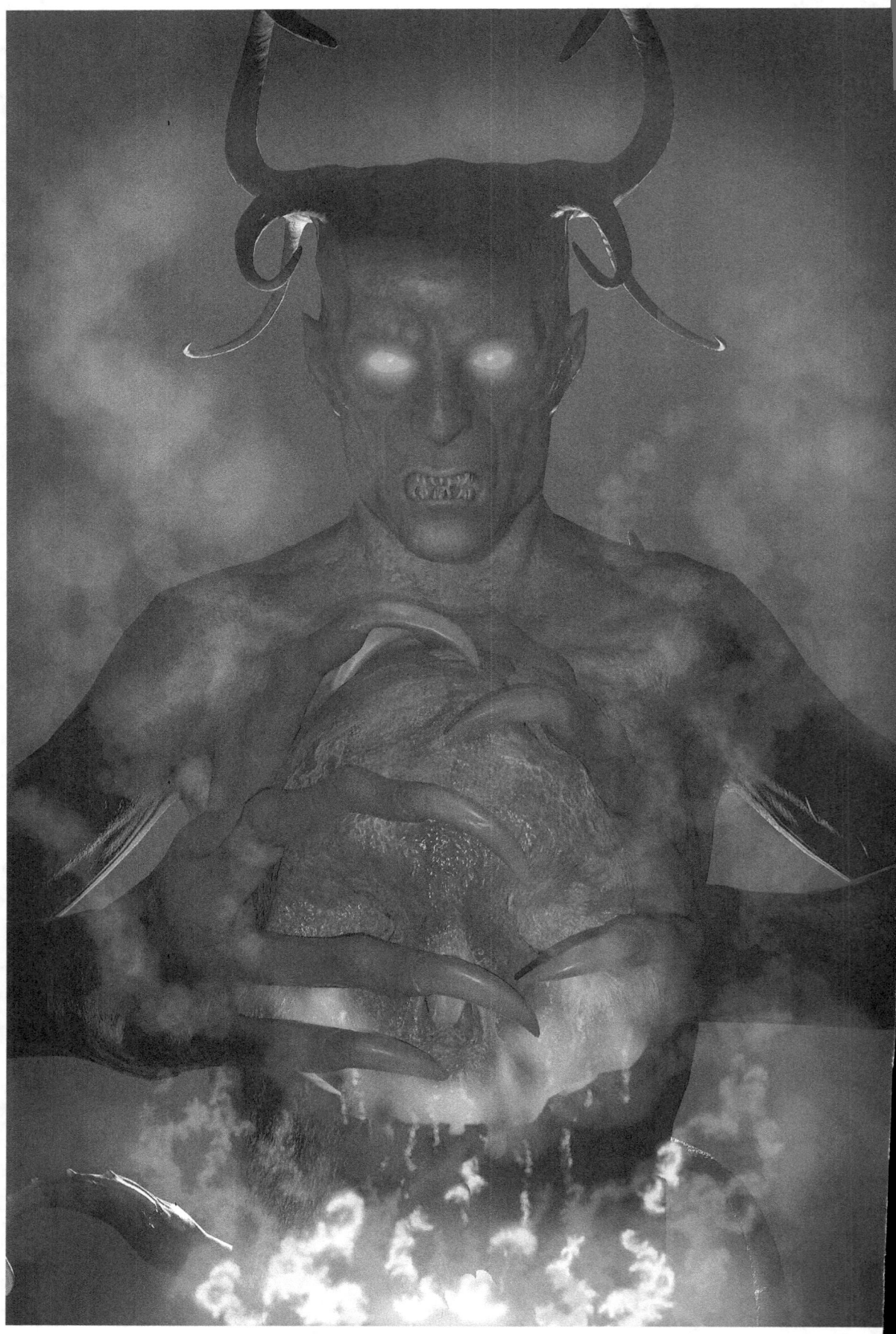

A WORD FROM THE PRESIDENT

Welcome to issue 17 of the AHWA flagship publication, *Midnight Echo*. Ex-president and all-around horror legend, Greg Chapman, is our guest editor this time and has put together a stellar issue. We're honoured to have his name on this one. I'm always so impressed with the depth and breadth of horror from Australasian writers. I've said it before, we punch way above our weight in this genre. It's no exaggeration—at least, I don't believe it is—to say that some of the best horror and dark fiction writers in the world come from this region. And I think the AHWA can give itself a little pat on the back for encouraging and supporting that and, just maybe, giving some of them an early boost in this very magazine. We don't publish often, usually only once a year (though it would be nice to increase that) but we do publish quality. Every single time this magazine is published, it showcases amazing talent. This issue is no different. Read these yarns, watch these authors—they're the people you'll see go from strength to strength in the world of horror. And we're very proud to have them.

Alan Baxter, President AHWA, NSW, July 2022

EDITORIAL

Once, a few years ago, I was at a small writing event in my hometown of Rockhampton when an attendee asked me, "What do you write?"

Of course, I answered with, "I'm a horror writer." The person's immediate reaction was to grimace and walk away. At first, this bothered me, but then I quickly understood her reaction was typical of someone who didn't *get* horror.

Horror fiction is more than blood and guts. Horror fiction, at its finest, concerns what it means to be *human*. By placing real (albeit fictional) people in strange, terrifying, or macabre situations, we discover who the characters truly are, and, in turn the reader might learn something about themselves as well.

I've been writing and publishing horror fiction for more than a decade, but this is my very first foray into the role of editor. When I was asked what the theme of my issue would be, I wanted authors to get to the *heart* of horror, to show me the versatility of the genre and more importantly, to make me *feel*—not just scared, but what it means to be human.

The stories you will read in this issue are by authors who *get* the horror genre and the horror short form. Within these pages you'll meet characters who are tormented physically and mentally, you'll meet others who find themselves in inexplicable situations, or encounter otherworldly terrors. The circumstances may be wildly imaginative, but the reality lies in the characters themselves. Because horror's true power isn't blood and guts—its power lies in its humanity.

I'd like to thank the authors for making my first foray into editing so enjoyable and effortless. Your stories are truly fantastic. I'd also like to thank the Australasian Horror Writers Association for this opportunity. I'm very glad my first foray was for them.

I hope you enjoy the issue.

Greg Chapman
Guest Editor, Midnight Echo Issue 17
Brisbane, July, 2022

LA BELLE MORTE SANS MERCI
BY KAT CLAY

As all deviancies do, it began in childhood.

1893 was the height of modernity—photographic technologies proliferated across the continent. The result? An explosive need to document oneself and one's family, even in death. Studios sprang up across London. My father was one such photographer by trade, his studio in a brick building near St. Pancras. From a young age I was apprenticed in his craft.

I opened the doors for women dressed in black lace veils hiding forbidden tears as they clutched bundles of baptismal clothes. I made strange pleasantries with these grieving mothers, death a void in which no conversation could foster, save that of the weeds of weather observations. I plugged my nose with smelling salts to pose their stillborn children in wooden cradles. All under the watchful eye of my father, who would punish me as soon as they had gone, for some slight I had not known existed.

My father was a strict man; my mother had gone beyond the immortal veil, leaving me with a man who knew only of his trade, and the necessity of cleanliness and purity in an increasingly amoral world. Small crimes under his watchful gaze—removing the processing chemicals recklessly, sitting before offering his clients a cup of tea, holding my limbs askew while standing and waiting for the exposure to finish—met with varying punishments. Mostly, he forced me to scrub the studio with chemicals until my hands burned. Sometimes, he locked me in the basement with the dead. And sometimes, I imagined I could hear them call to me in the pitch dark, their hands pulling me down to Sheol.

Through these strange portraits I became obsessed with mortality—the living and the dead, but especially that which lay between. Decay fascinated me. The rotting of a fallen log, the rind of green mould upon an old orange. We are all dying, but none of us acknowledges this truth; instead, we parade as if immortality is our guarantee. None of us wish to acknowledge the white strands amongst black hair or the lines around our eyes.

As a teenager, my father's obsession with cleanliness escalated into hours of revival meetings with the Hallelujah Lasses of the Salvation Army, banging their tambourines on bicycles, espousing the perils of drink on the cobblestoned streets of London. I too stood behind him at these meetings, feeling increasingly at odds with the Salvationists and what I saw daily. What did God say about the dead babies in their baptismal clothes?

Knowing what I do now, it was all too true. I should have stayed there and joined William Booth's army of evangelists. Instead, I lingered too long in a city that should be destroyed.

After hours, I began seeking answers to the great question—WHY—in photographic subjects who presented evidence of death on earth. They held the key to suffering and sin. Why would a just God allow his children to suffer? Was it only a by-product of the decaying world around us? Could we not escape this fate through doing good?

Rumours gleaned from Ratcliffe Highway whores led me to my first subject: a woman whose blood emanated from her lungs in heaving clots. Her face a blur on the film as she retched into a handkerchief, stained red with sputum. Had she done ill in life to end up so? I asked her husband, who said nothing and ground his teeth into a tobacco pipe.

I wanted more. A viscerality that was not present when the decay was internal. Through my contacts I found a man whose leg was being eaten by maggots as he lived; purple putrescent skin in which those white worms wriggled. I hid my pleasure at his disease. This was exactly what I had sought—those who wore their sins on their skin. He must have done something terrible in life to end up so, but when I enquired as to his life, he was a man of simplicity—he had worked, attended church, grown a family, and soon to death he would go. I processed those negatives with a giddy pleasure. And yet, something was missing.

I threw myself into my work, tumbling deeper down the alleys of the East End, where the city's smog sat heavy on homes coated with a film of soot. Bribing cutpurses and dollymops, I found a woman whose breasts had turned black with cancerous growth. I went to threshing houses and photographed the backs of prostitutes after the clients had finished, thick red welts upon their bodies. I stumbled through the aisles of the Royal Free Hospital under the guise of being a medical student, all the while tantalising those wretches with the promise of money to pose for me. With each photograph, I

was moving closer to and yet further away from my mission: that of pure decay.

And then I heard of the Veil.

She had no name, nor was she the Woman in the Veil, some melodramatic take on a Wilkie Collins penny dreadful. Simply, *the Veil*.

When I enquired as to her namesake around the harlot traps, one woman's response was, "No one knows what lies underneath, sir. She ain't never taken it off, not for nothing, not even a John. They say all who see her face ends up dead, but still they come to Hyde Park, and still them pervs get out them willies and fuck her. They want to know what's underneath, but they don't realise it ain't found down there. So, what'll it be, sir? No need to go to Hyde Park. If that's your fancy, I'll put on a scarf and you can do me right here."

But her voice was lost in the dark as I hailed a cab, with only dim lamplight to guide Charon in the dark.

***

What is beautiful by day is deadly in the night. Hyde Park was one such place: the genteel would walk its leafy ways through the day, tipping hats to one another. By night, Hyde Park was a den of debauchery—as soon as the sun set, it became the haunt of night walkers and profligates. And so, I joined them.

My first visit to Hyde Park was fruitless; all that could be heard in the night was the huffing of bodies upon one another. While I waited and walked the grounds, clad in a dark cloak, I sometimes watched these sexual encounters—clothed, unclothed, men and women, men and men, women and women, and more. Sex was decay, both a lust and disdain for death caught up in that moment of copulation.

In those next visits, I learned the groves and glades popular for these illicit encounters and arrived early, setting up my camera silently in beds of lilies and irises so admired by the gentility in the day. And yet she did not come. The vivid memories of these nocturnal sins disappeared on film, the lens too slow, the exposures too blurry. Film could not represent the reality of these depraved individuals.

One night, when wet grass grew heavy under the weight of rain and water dripped from the bowed branches of fir trees, I came across a hidden pool, a marble mausoleum at its end. I had been certain I had traced every corner of the park, and yet here, when I was lost in thought, did I stumble on this eerie place. While ripples bounded in the puddles on the track, none fell in the still water of the long pool. It was then I knew I would find the Veil; it was here she lived, in the shadows of that mausoleum.

She emerged from the doorway of the tomb. I did not know where the shadows ended and her figure began, dressed as she was all in black. It was as if she were in mourning for someone, and I asked her this, using the charms I had gathered from wooing aged mothers.

"Who do you mourn for?"

In the faint glimmer of the gibbous moon, I could only perceive through her veil dimly, but I imagined the upwards turn of her lips as she said, "I mourn for you."

Her answer took me aback, for I was a virile man in the prime of my life. But I held my ground as she edged closer, her pale fingers trailing along the marble. Fine black dentelle lace ran along the edges of her veil, in patterns that swirled in upon each other the closer she got to me. Yet her odour reached me first; that erotic scent of decaying flesh I had learned so faithfully from the Whitechapel slums. It called to me. All I wanted to do was reach my fingertips to the bottom of that veil and devour the abyss. Something stopped me; perhaps it was the warning that all who see her face die.

"Will you sit for me and be photographed?" I asked, gesturing to the camera and tripod under my arms.

She tilted her head ever slightly upwards; the veil catching the light of the moon through a broken rain cloud. She examined me, circumnavigating my body at a distance, testing me for some purpose unknown.

The more I tried to parse what lay underneath, the more her veil became diaphanous. It was deliberately obfuscating me, and so was she.

"What do you hope to gain from capturing my image?" she said.

I hesitated. Here was a woman who lived the line between life and death. I could smell it on her—the sweet perfume of lilies masking the effluvia of bereavement.

"It might seem like a simplistic question, but I have sought the answer to it all my life in the captured image. Why do people suffer?"

She laughed, a curt sound. "A photograph cannot answer that question. It is a still moment in time, and suffering is eternal. Take a simple image of these flowers," she said, gesturing to a bed of white poppies. "They are the flower of death. Their milk can ease pain; too much, and it causes the death it symbolises. But they too wilt and die. How much more so the pain and suffering of humans? You seek to photograph me in my decay, but did you capture all the moments that led here?"

"Yet if I photograph the flowers, they will not die. They will always exist even when they cease to go on living."

"A photograph is no better than the dead—caught, frozen, still."

"You are coy, woman. I have heard from the streets of London that you know its secrets. All who see your face die. And so, I wish to photograph it."

She laughed, and with it carried the rasp a gramophone makes when the needle is laid upon a tune.

"It is so silly," she said, pulling me towards the mausoleum pool, tantalising me with a hint of lifted skirt. "Do you not realise that all who see your face die? We are all dying. But I will show you what lies beyond my veil."

She knelt beside the pool, her reflection pristine in the calm. Not a ripple, nor a leaf, broke the water's surface. All the while, her veil did not slip once, even when gravity demanded its due. She gestured for me to gaze at my reflection.

The surface had erased my face, a blur of movement on a still lake. And in looking at that pool, I had the sensation I was looking at her. I reached towards her veil, my fingers tipping up the edge of that fine lace. But was that her reflection in the water, or her true self?

Without warning, clawed fingers grabbed the back of my head and pushed it face first into that pool. The ice water shocked any fatigue from my body; eyes wide, I saw everything in that darkness. An abyss opened, and I stepped through.

My father spoke of the Thames before the great cholera epidemic; a canker of open sewage that left a miasma over the city. This water was pure and putrescent. I could see everything, yet bile gorged in my throat. As my eyes adjusted, I made out shapes within the water; two white, ghostly hands reached for my face from the darkness. When they grew closer, the decay on their hands was visible; these were not ghost hands but the hands of the dead, soaked in water until the skin slipped away from their bones.

I opened my mouth to scream. It filled with water flecked with the skin. I would drown here if I did not stop her.

When I tried to grab her hand, she slapped me away, her fingers firmer than my expectations for any woman. The dead hands grew closer. I had wished to see decay, and here it was. For any man, it would have scared them back to the comfort of a quiet life, but I had glimpsed the world beyond this one. The answers to my questions were so close and yet so far. Heaving with every effort, I pushed back against the stone edge of the pool, my head breaching for air with a mighty heave.

I rolled over and stared at the sky, exhausted as if from a sexual encounter. The rain clouds had parted for one moment to reveal the brilliance of stars. When I blinked, bleak clouds had consumed each pinpoint of light. Nothing remained in the heavens.

And in the disappearance of the stars, so too had she left me.

***

My obsession with decay took a swift turn into an obsession with *her*. Uncovering the Veil would be the epitome of my work. If only I could see what was underneath, I became convinced that I would open some great secret of the world.

I spent my waking hours walking Hyde Park, akin to a ghost, wandering until the gates closed at 10pm. Even then, I hid within bushes and gardens from the gatekeeper to find that desolate pool once more, and with it, the keeper of the mausoleum.

She eluded me, as most women did.

My Hyde Park meanderings did not go unnoticed by my employer; when I turned up to work late for several days, fatigued from my explorations, he sent me packing. What reliable work I had was now gone, and with no funds to pay my rental, I sold my furniture to pay my debts. The cabinet my father had given me when I left home; the bed I had purchased with my first pay; and finally, the locket which held the last memory of my mother.

Yet I still held my camera dearly, as my record keeper of the vile. I walked the streets, a ghost myself, hungry and fatigued, until I could not afford even a shared bedsit filled with lice. Forced by desperation, I took work in Holywell Street, that degenerate lane transformed from clothing shops to pornographic publishers. Each window advertised their wares. Books of women in lewd positions, with other men and women, sometimes wrapped in the throes of orgy. There are those who take issue with such displays, who write to the *Times* over such publications, and I have wondered through the years how they might know of such degeneracy, if they had not been here themselves.

In my humble defence, my interest in decay was an honest one. Honest, because so many people in our society refuse to acknowledge their desires for the sake of moral propriety. I started with images of women; corsets knotted so tightly they left bruises on their rib cages when removed. I was drawn to the flesh as moth to a flame, hiding myself under the black photographer's tent to expose all.

I spent days thumping my fist in my pants underneath the camera's velvet veil, until I abandoned my cover to include myself in these images, sometimes watching, sometimes centring myself as a subject of these photographs. All the while, so ashamed of what I had become. Where was that young boy who had politely made tea for grieving mothers? I abhorred myself yet could not escape the void I had entered. The hands of the dead dragged me into the abyss of life.

Pursuit by the Society for the Suppression of Vice forced me underground, to a less seemly establishment out of the prying eyes of those crusading proselytisers for morality. It was here I encountered the Veil once more; throwing black lace over the faces of desperate women, their bodies bound with mourning clothes or sometimes nothing at all, trying to recognise if any of these might be that which I sought. But all fell short. These were imitations of a woman I had once met. She tortured me in her absence; a void, much like the depths underneath that dark skirt.

Yet she did not leave me.

It was three years after this depravity that I began my transformation.

***

It started as a pox upon my genitals. Lumpen papules spared no quarter of my skin. What had I done that had demanded such visibility of my sins?

At the same time as my repulsion to myself, I felt a strange obsession with my corpse. Each day, I examined every quarter of my flesh. Here was the decay I had so longed to photograph, yet I could not bring myself to photograph my downfall. Distance was key. I was not like those people I photographed. They had done wrong. They wore their sins on their skin.

It came to a point that even the whores I hired recoiled from my body.

"You got the ladies' disease," said one of the girls. "Syphilis. There's doctors that got treatments for it, but for that you need lots of money. And neither of us got none of that."

From these terrible wounds, my body burned with fever. I shivered and sweated alone in bed, with no friend to care for me, no housekeeper, just a landlord who threatened to throw me out if I didn't get back to making the pornography that kept him in business. I used the tripod to lever myself out of bed and collapsed with the camera in my hands.

Time passed and then it did not.

Fever consumed me. In my delirium, I flew high above London, so high that the stars might absorb my body to heaven itself. Until I could soar no longer, falling without control to the perilous spires of the decaying city itself. Plummeting to the cobblestones, those dead, watery hands reached for me, swallowing me into the earth's abyss.

Pain subsumed my body, as if my bones were breaking from that heavenly fall. My torture of hell—to be broken and re-knit, for defying the sanctity of the bodily temple.

In the fever's passing, the sores travelled to the extremities of my body, covering my face with raised lumps. I tried burning them with the end of a cigarillo, searing them with flame. They only exploded deep yellow pus, leaving burn marks and open wounds that cankered into infection.

Before long, they ate my body from the inside out, great ulcers forming along my gums, eating away at the skin. Two teeth fell out, nothing to keep them in my mouth. I placed them on the sink as trophies of my decay.

At the absence of my regular letters cajoling money, my father searched me out—whether it was from concern or disdain I know not to this day.

"You've brought shame on all of us. Better that you were dead and with the saints, and not this abscess of a human being. You had a choice between the man you could be and the man you have become, and you embraced sin rather than rejected it."

As sons disappeared from their fathers, so our bond of kin had decayed.

Instead, he took my camera from its sacred stand in my room. I, too weak to stop him, reached and fell out of bed. It was too late.

On his return, he brought with him a meagre bundle of notes and two men in white uniforms. "Not those archangels!" I shouted as they carted me into their ambulance. The last vision of my father: his face turned away as his messengers shut me out from paradise.

***

The asylum was a dank, skittering place. The sound of rats inhabited the walls. I wondered if they were rats at all, or my imagination, but I woke once to find one nibbling at my feet, its terrible tongue negotiating the open wounds on my body. I shook it off and tried to kill it, but it was too fast, and it returned to the walls from where it came.

"Have you seen the woman known only as the Veil?" I asked my fellow men, for they knew the whisperings of God. They talked of Him constantly, in the house of sanity. "No, I have not, but as surely I would like to know her," said Joseph Picton, a painter. He killed seven women and was in Bedlam for that very reason, but I believed he was an artist and knew something of that which I sought. "All women are the devil," he said. "I am a holy man and wish to rid them from this world. What ho, your treatments are here."

The archangels surrounded me—men in white gowns ready to drag me away. Would that they took me to hell so that I could photograph each precious victim! But they dragged me to my personal torture chamber. The men tied me down and stripped my pants off, exposing the seeping wounds on my legs and member, pustules bursting like those very mushrooms I admired.

The doctor took my flaccid, lumpen penis in his hands—it stiffened at his touch—until he lifted a hypodermic syringe full of a strange metallic liquid. I watched it as it moved, as if it had a life of its own within that vial, intoxicating and—pain! The doctor injected the needle into my urethra. Miasma seeped through my member, and it was as if I was in the void under the veil and she was there with me, and I knew it will not be long before I see her again.

I started this journey in search of the great question–WHY? A question spurred by the suffering of innocent mothers in their grief. Now I turned the question upon myself. Why was I born if only to suffer? Was it my destiny or my choice that I ended my days in this sanitorium, on a slab, a doctor staring at my genitals with disdain and judgement? It was the same look that I gave to those I photographed, and now he looked upon me. It was torture, this procedure, made worse by the look upon that man's face, that I was not a man at all but a human-shaped growth, a fungus on this earth, something to be cleansed and purified with chemicals so that no rot would grow again.

In the days after, my forehead swelled with sores. I despised myself for my choices. I had two selves—one good, one evil—and had chosen the latter for my life. Overwhelmed by a need to destroy my sinful flesh, I clawed at my cheeks, ripping off shreds of skin. Perhaps the veil was within me, and in looking inside myself, I could see what was underneath. But the mirrors in that place were grimy and did not show me my true nature, for there was no veil, only a void where my skin once was, my teeth borne out as my gums receded and my mouth was eaten away by itself. I ripped my weakened nose from my face and stared at it in my hand, and back into the remaining cavity. Still, I could not see myself properly.

"You can make a camera with almost anything," I whispered to Picton as he painted me. When my portrait was complete, he revealed it. Who was this monster with a missing nose and decayed face? I threw the picture across the room and the oil paint smeared with straw and faeces.

No, what I needed was a camera obscura—the dark chamber. It was the only thing that could truly illuminate me.

I scavenged materials from my colleagues when they were not looking, for we were allowed out of our chambers during the day. A box and gelatin from the kitchen, a flint and candle from the larder, silver chloride and paper from the dispensary, and a nail from one of Picton's frames when he was not looking. It was with this I punched a hole in the box's front.

"What do you see?" I said to the box as I struck the flint upon the candle wick in the dead of night.

The camera did not reply for a long time, mulling over its response. I was still, so still, for what was an hour, what was a lifetime. Finally, the camera replied with my face upside down, reversed, upon the paper. I held it to the light.

For one moment, I glimpsed a true vision of myself: I was not a man but a void.

Too late I had my answer to the question–WHY? Terrible things can happen to us in life, but our response to those events is always a choice. It was not God who caused these disasters, but the existence of sin itself. The world was in a constant state of decay; everywhere I looked, from the mould on the walls to my own putrid body. I could have helped those I came across in their pain. Instead, I was a vector of suffering, using their images for my own selfish pursuit.

Where my father turned to God, I turned away. My entire life has been a crossing of moral thresholds, one veil after another. We may say that one temptation will satisfy, but there is another around the corner, until I have found myself in the very abscess I sought to photograph.

I only wish I had turned the camera upon myself earlier.

The print of my face slowly turned black as it was subjected to candlelight, until the entire paper coated in silver chloride was stained with its exposure.

In the days which followed my self-portrait, my body stiffened. Those fateful words she had uttered came back to haunt me. A photograph is no better than the dead—caught, frozen, still. And so, I discovered what it was to be a photograph, frozen in time. Syphilis paralysed me.

I lay on my cot with my box camera clutched in my hands, and if anyone tried to remove it, I screamed at them. If only I could find her and photograph her, my whole wretched life would have served some point.

My body froze. I watched the rain fall outside the window. Flecks hit my face. Someone should have closed that window, but I could not reach. I could no longer tell reality from illusion. Madness consumed me. Day passed and turned to night and day and day and night. The stars fell like little beams of light, which turned to shards of glass and cut me.

On this night of these falling stars, my breath stilled, and she came to me.

I was in Hyde Park again, near that pool in which no rain fell. The sight of that calm water stilled my mind. Yet the light was different; in life, I could see that dreaded mausoleum, but through a veil dimly. Now I was on the other side, viewing the world from underneath the water. Others called to me unseen from the depths, for the pool had no visible bottom, only darkness. There was a sense of both terror and wonder there. This world was beyond all that I experienced in life, yet it was the grandeur of that great abyss that terrified me. I felt the same stupefied exhaustion as on the night I first investigated this pool.

Desperate to reach land, I kicked my feet towards the light. And yet, the oppressive water dragged me under.

It was then she came to me. A veiled face

broke through the stillness of the surface. She floated towards me, as if on air, her dress languid. All the while, I could not see her face. Here, her veil was water, lit from behind. It stretched longer than my fingers could lift.

If only I could see what lay beyond, perhaps I would not drown. Perhaps I would have my second chance at the light. Striving, I reached a white, decaying hand towards the edge of that cursed veil. It was as fickle as water itself.

One hand, then two, placed upon that fine netting, my destiny underneath, the black liquid tipped upwards, the hint of a white neck, grasping, groping, forever trying to see what was underneath.

And yet, my dead hands could not raise it. We were trapped in a curiosity loop—as I lifted, she leaned away. Still, I needed to see what lay beyond, if only to understand why.

I grabbed for the edges, desperate, and with the last mite of my strength, lifted the veil.

What I found was not a woman's face, but one that I had been intimately familiar. I knew every ridge and crevasse, every weary line, every hair of that which I had been before I devolved into this hideous being.

It was my face the night I met the Veil. Those ghastly fingers I had recoiled from in the pool were my own. Oh, why hadn't I heeded my warning? WHY?

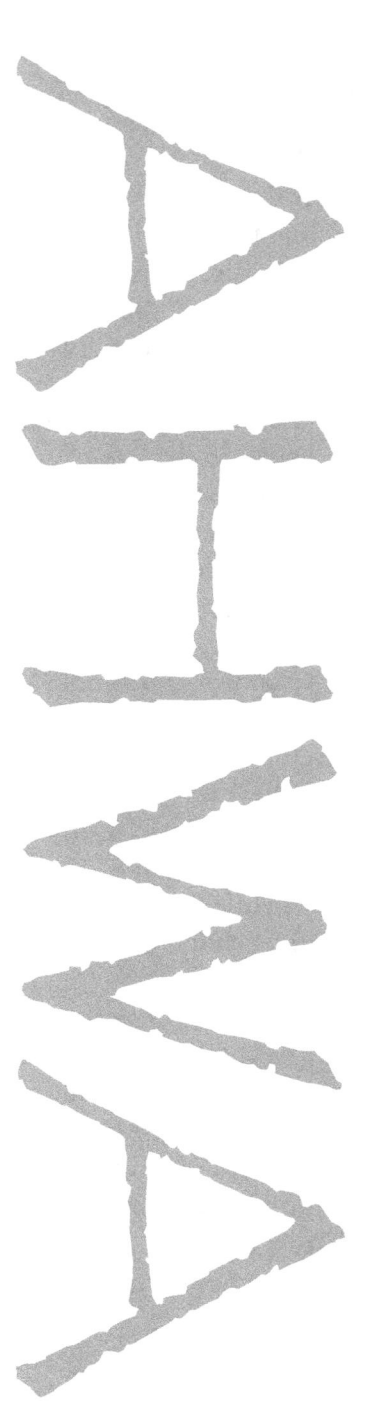

SMOTHERED, STILL AND SILENT
BY DEBORAH SHELDON

Floodwaters lap at my house all night long,
Sopping, sighing. Electricity out,
Home so quiet. Morning brings no birdsong
And I open the curtains, look about,
See no sign of water. Instead: whiteout.
Snow across my property, trees and lawn.
Snow in autumn? How? Shocked, I want to shout.
Utter silence. The world's noises are gone.

No barking dogs, no trill of currajong,
No sound of neighbours. I begin to doubt...
Snow? I lift the window and flinch. Strong,
Musky stink – sweet, sick and rancid – has clout.
Wait! There, floating on the breeze, a great rout
Of spiders in their millions, threads airborne.
"Snow" is webs; landed after the washout.
Utter silence. The world's noises are gone.

Panicked, I drive from the garage. If wrong,
Then fleeing my house does nothing but out
Me as a coward. So what? Through the throng
Of webs I force my car, taking the route
To town. Clogged roads as far as I can scout.
Kerbside, cocooned vehicles. This white dawn
Is death. Spiders breach my car. Webs sprout.
Utter silence. The world's noises are gone.

I try to pray; I've never been devout.
Spiders spin mesh around my head, stick on
Eyes. Lips. Ears. I thrash like a landed trout.
Utter silence. The world's noises are gone.

FEATHERS
BY CHRIS MASON

The latch on the front door clicked, followed by the sound of keys clinking against the bottom of the bowl on the hallstand. Sophie poked her head out of the nursery. The front door was shut and the hallway empty. Damn it, her mind was playing tricks on her again. What did they call it? Brain fog? Wishful thinking? Delusion? Was it any wonder she was confused? It was tough living alone. The house was far too big, and far too quiet. She wasn't supposed to be pregnant. Nope. Being a mummy had definitely *not* been on her 'to do' list. Eric wasn't supposed to be dead either. Sophie groaned. How was she expected to do this on her own? And how much more shit was life going to chuck at her? *Fuck!*

She rubbed her brow with the back of her hand, leaving a smear of sweat and grime. What the hell was she doing? Ah yes, pretending everything was fine. Normal. Like it was before she couldn't see her toes. She reached and grabbed a corner of wallpaper. A twinge in her lower back reminded her to go easy. Almost there. The last sheet of paper came away with a chunk of plaster and a blob of ancient glue that looked like amber.

Sophie stepped back. Good news. No creepy kid's drawings, satanic symbols, or 'GET OUT' warnings scrawled in blood. Eric would have been disappointed. He'd been convinced they'd find something evil lurking once they started pulling the house apart. *This place hates me*, he'd said when—not long after they'd bought it—they found out the plumbing leaked, and the wiring was stuffed. "Old houses," said Sophie. "Just you wait and see, it'll be beautiful one day. Worth every penny."

She studied the naked wall. The plaster had a few cracks. A bit of filler and a light sand would fix them. Then a couple of coats of paint. It was a big job. Leaving it to the last minute wasn't the smartest thing she'd ever done, but she still had a week before the baby was due. Sophie patted her stomach. It was stretched to the limit under a stained t-shirt. "You're going to give me a few more days to finish this aren't you, buddy?" The reply came in the form of a foot kicking up under her ribcage. She hitched in a breath. "Yeah, I know. It's getting tight in there."

Not long after they'd married, Sophie and Eric had two important conversations. The first was about children. Eric was on the fence, but Sophie had been adamant. There'd be no kids. She wasn't the maternal type. More to the point, she didn't want to put herself in a position where she might repeat the mistakes of the past. Her parents hadn't been what you'd call… invested. After their divorce, Sophie,— then eleven—had barely qualified as an afterthought. No amount of money made up for the harsh reality that both her mother and father wanted to move on without her. There was no invite to where they were going. Ireland, in the case of her father, and a second marriage for her mother. In the end, boarding school hadn't been awful. In her final year, she'd met Eric.

The second conversation was a follow-on from a promise to grow old together. Sophie and Eric decided whoever died first and discovered there was an afterlife, would send the other a white feather as proof. Not an original idea, but who cared. If it worked, it worked. Looking back, it was silly to want to extend their love beyond the bounds of what they already had. And what they'd had was damn near perfect. All moot now, of course. With Eric gone seven months already, Sophie wasn't holding out on him keeping his end of the bargain. Pigeons dropped their grey feathers in the yard, galahs left little pink ones. She even found a bright green feather, gifted by a chatty lorikeet dining on the nectar of the pussy willow at the side of the house. Nothing from the corellas and sulphur crested cockatoos though. Not one fucking feather. Miserable bastards. It seemed death was a big black hole after all. And yet… her mind continued to tease her.

It took most of the next day for Sophie to prep the walls for painting. She took her time scraping back ridges of plaster, ensuring the surface was even. It was what Eric would have done. He'd been good with detail. Sophie, not so much. But if there was going to be one finished room in this house, it was going to be done properly. A nursery for their son. She could at least give Eric that. *I was going to tell you… it's just, I needed time to get used to the idea. And I have. I really have.*

"You know that, right? Eric? I do want this baby," said Sophie.

Silence.

Who was she kidding? He wasn't there.

"Is anyone listening? *Anyone? Someone?*" Damn, it was lonely. Her world had been small with Eric. It had grown even smaller without him. She had no siblings, rarely saw her neighbours (probably a blessing), and she hadn't worked since COVID caused her café to close. Her two dearest friends—her only friends—were in Bali for a 'destination' wedding and extended holiday. If she hadn't been the size of a bus, Sophie might have joined them. But then it would have felt wrong; too soon to have any kind of fun when her husband's ashes were sitting in a box beside the bed.

By three in the afternoon, Sophie had vacuumed up the plaster dust and was ready to paint. Her stomach growled. Lunch seemed like hours ago. It had consisted of coffee and three slices of raisin toast. She could have gone an extra slice but had opted to play it safe. At this late stage of her pregnancy, it was a miracle she was able to digest anything at all. Especially when there was a future world champion kick boxer inside her competing for space with her major organs. Sophie's belly undulated as a hand… a foot… an elbow… or whatever punched a trail from left to right. "Settle down in there, little guy," she cooed. Her nose wrinkled. God, when had she started to sound like… like a mother?

She made a trip to the toilet, peed in intermittent bursts, then went back to the nursery. *Okay, let's get this first coat done.* She dipped a roller on a stick into a tray of paint. The colour she'd chosen was a pale mint green. Together with the white ceiling and woodwork, the green would make the room feel lighter. The floral print she'd ripped from the walls had screamed seventies. Loops of pinks and orange. Sophie wanted calm. She *would* be calm. She *had* to remain calm. The latch on the front door clicked. This time she ignored it. Eric wasn't coming back no matter how much she wanted him too.

By five o'clock, Sophie had finished with the roller and cut in around the edges with a brush. She covered the roller in plastic wrap and dropped the brush into a bucket of water. It was enough for today. Her back and shoulders were on fire. If she could get in and out of a bath without killing herself, she would have. Instead, she stood under a hot shower for a full twenty minutes, watching water spill over the deep purple stretch marks on her stomach. Oh, the joys of pregnancy.

Sophie ate a small bowl of pasta for dinner. Then half a block of dark chocolate washed down with a steaming mug of Milo. If she was going to be up all night with food repeating on her she may as well eat something she enjoyed. She propped herself up on the sofa, one cushion shoved into her lower back, another between her knees. Two episodes of *Ozark*, and her eyes were heavy. Despite their best efforts, Marty and Wendy Byrd couldn't hold her interest. Half asleep, she padded down the hallway towards the bedroom. On the way she made a quick detour into the nursery. She was pleased with her efforts. It was amazing how something as simple as a lick of paint could transform a room. Another day and it would be done. She opened the window to let fresh air in and the smell of paint out then closed the door behind her.

Around one in the morning, Sophie needed to pee. The bathroom was across the hall from the nursery. She yawned as she flushed the toilet. The tiles were cold on her feet. Slippers, she reminded herself. Above the sink, a mirror reflected the dark hallway and a rectangle washed in grey. Sophie turned and frowned. The door to the nursery was wide open.

Sophie reached for the light switch inside the door and snapped it on. The green walls leaped to life. A stiff breeze blew through the window. Always a rational explanation, thought Sophie. She hadn't closed the door properly and the breeze had caused it to swing open. She crossed the room and pulled the sash window down. Her eyes flicked to each corner of the room. No feather. It didn't surprise her. She closed the door, gave it an extra pull to ensure it would stay that way, and waddled back to bed.

She slept in until ten. There was a message on her phone from her mother. The usual. *I'm worried. I'd feel better if you came home. Stay for as long as you like. I can hire a nanny. I think that would be best, don't you?* She didn't call anymore because Sophie never picked up. Why would she? There was no point thinking it was in any way possible to salvage their relationship after what had passed between them. If Sophie thought for one minute guilt played a part in the equation, which it didn't, she might have caved. The sudden interest in being a grandmother was entirely performative. Nicole Beckett-Coleman's ability to make everything about herself was, without a doubt, impressive. Every day, Sophie thanked God that Eric's job had taken them interstate. She texted back, *I'M FINE!* and threw the phone onto the dresser.

The door to the nursery was open. Again. She looked away then back at the door. Still open. Not her imagination. Sophie entered the room. A stain on the far wall caught her immediate attention. It stretched from ceiling to floor—a smoky grey mark that split in two halfway down, like elongated legs standing on tippytoe. *You have got to be kidding me. What now?* Surely not a leak in the roof, not after they'd spent a fortune replacing it a year ago. She ran her hand down the wall, feeling for dampness. The paint was dry. She traced a finger around the edge of the stain. Was there mould in the plaster that had leached through? Forget the door, this was serious. Toxic mould! What every pair of newborn lungs needed. She stretched her arms above her head, feeling each joint click. There was only one thing for it—more elbow grease. She went to the kitchen, grabbed a bottle of bleach and a mask, then scrubbed the plaster. The stain faded to a fuzzy outline. If she put the second coat on nice and thick, it would cover. She poured paint into a tray and went to work.

The next day, the stain was back. Sophie put a third coat of paint on the offending wall. By the afternoon, it was obvious the problem wasn't going away. It was worse. Darker and wider, the stain now resembled something vaguely human— wide shoulders, thick arms, a head, and impossibly long legs.

Sophie's phone vibrated in the pocket of her trackpants. Another text message from her mother. *I've booked a flight for tomorrow. I get in around four. I suppose you're in no condition to drive, so I'll get a taxi from the airport.*

Close to tears, Sophie didn't need this distraction now. Her fingers skipped across the screen. *Don't come. Cancel the flight.* She sighed and stared at the figure on the wall. In the womb, her baby shifted. The bulge in her stomach was lower than the day before. For a split-second, she thought she saw the shape on the wall bulge too.

Eric? It had to be, didn't it? Not a feather, but a grand entrance for the arrival of their baby. She texted: *Mum, no need to panic. I'm not here alone.* And hoped to hell she was right. The alternative didn't bear thinking about.

In the kitchen, Sophie leaned forward on the counter with her legs apart. It was the most comfortable position she could find. She rocked her hips from side to side. There was no pain but the weight on her pelvis was undeniable. She rubbed her stomach and thought about the night of the accident. It had been raining. The petrol tanker, which Eric probably didn't see until it was too late, had run a red light. On the downhill run of the freeway, brakes failing, the tanker was never going to stop. Eric had no chance. It was impossible to know if he survived the crash. Sophie tried not to go there, because he certainly had not survived the inferno. He was always home from work by six. The police knocked on her door at eight. They didn't have to say a thing. She'd already seen it on the news. She knew Eric was dead. Felt it in her bones. It made sense. It all made sense. *I should have told him about the baby.*

That night there was little sleep for Sophie. She found it hard to sit for any length of time and bed offered no comfort. Although her body wanted rest, searching for the most comfortable position on the sofa, her mind was unwilling to give in. It flitted from one thing to another. In between making banal lists of what was yet to be done before the impending birth, and excitement about the ghost in the wall, she dozed on and off. The rest of the time she slow-walked through the house, pausing regularly to lean against pieces of furniture. The door to the nursery refused to stay closed. As the night wore on the figure on the wall grew sharper. She didn't go into the room. Confused about what she was experiencing—a lucid dream, or a miracle? —she hovered in the doorway, not wanting to break the spell. The lights in the hallway cast a wedge of soft gold across to the far wall of the nursery. There were elbows and fingers now, the chest and abdomen clearly defined. Towards dawn, the hollow of a mouth appeared and then the glint of an eye. Sophie held back from rushing into the room. *Be patient, wait a little longer.* When he was fully formed and drenched in sunlight, she'd go to him. Fall into his embrace.

Her body and mind exhausted, Sophie finally crawled into bed. She could rest now. There was nothing more to be done. Her beloved was home at last. She had called to him, and he had come. No feather required.

Sophie woke with a start several hours later. The air was cold, and a steady rain beat against the window. Every muscle in her body ached. Shivering, she crossed the hallway to the nursery. As she entered the room, her breath caught in her throat. The pale green walls were featureless. No stain. No imprint. No Eric, waiting.

The latch on the front door clicked. Keys clinked in the bottom of the bowl on the hallstand. She spun round, tears flowing.

Something skittered across the ceiling. High on the opposite wall, a crack appeared. A shadow crept from it, slick as smoke.

Frightened, Sophie backed into the far corner. The baby inside her lay still. She felt light-headed, nauseous. This wasn't right. Not how it was supposed to be.

From behind, she felt the wall flex, and a hot rancid breath on her neck. Strong hands reached under her thin cotton nightshirt and slid across her stomach. Her head turned in horror and she caught a flash of red eyes, furnace bright, set deep in a wicked face. A black tongue licked her ear… her cheek… extended snake-like to explore her mouth.

NO!

Panicked, she fought against thick ropy arms, holding her fast.

Her stomach cramped and she screamed.

Talons scraped the inside of her thigh, ripped into the flesh below her navel. Blood sprayed across walls, no longer calm but throbbing with menace.

Then all she knew was pain.

And all she saw were feathers, shiny and black, swirling across the floor.

WINNER OF THE
AUSTRALIAN SHADOWS AWARD
FOR BEST EDITED WORK 2020

ISSUE 15

MIDNIGHT
ECHO

EDITED BY
LEE MURRAY

Featuring
JOANNE ANDERTON
JAY CASELBERG
TOM DULLEMOND
JASON FRANKS
REBECCA FRASER
ANTHONY PAUL FERGUSON
J.A. HAIGH
MELANIE HARDING-SHAW
JULEIGH HOWARD-HOBSON
NIKKY LEE
MARTIN LIVINGS
STUART OLVER
DAVID SCHEMBRI
DEBORAH SHELDON
ALISSA SMITH

AHWA

The Magazine of the Australasian Horror Writers A

AHWA

HAND AND HEART
BY GERALDINE BORELLA

She wakes with a heaving gasp—a free-diver resurfacing—and clutches at her chest. There's no gaping hole there, no remnants of a skeletal hand plunging into her flesh, plucking her heart out, beating and bloodied.

Through ragged breaths, she moans.

"What...?" Gill grunts and rolls over, rubbing bleary eyes. "Not *another* nightmare?" Lauren nods, unable to speak. The words needed to explain the jolt and horror aren't there. With a huff, Gill tugs the sheet across to cover him, turning his back to her. "We've got to see Benjamin about this," he mutters.

"No," says Lauren. "We don't." She shakes her head, then swivels to plant her feet on the cool tiles. "I'm okay. Really."

"Don't be so goddamned stubborn," says Gill. He sits up and reaches for his glasses. "He can fix this. You know he can."

Lauren turns and glares. "Maybe I don't need to be fixed."

"Jesus, Lauren, denial will get you nowhere." As if to close off the conversation, he reaches for his latest published tome and flips through the glossy pages filled with photographs of endangered species. Meanwhile, Lauren pads off to the kitchen, coffee uppermost in mind.

Despite minor tiffs and irritations they've been lucky, protected from the travails a married couple might suffer. Lauren's grateful for it, pleased they agree on the important things. Like whether or not to have children. It's always been off the agenda, both too focussed on work to consider adding a child to the mix. Living remote, almost hermit-like, another mutual requirement. It saw them settle in the Daintree, north of Cairns, a place with a tenuous grip on its dwindling patch of 200 million year-old rainforest, providing inspiration for Lauren's landscape painting, wildlife for Gill to photograph, and trails for both to explore. An idyllic existence. Though lately—well, for Lauren, at least—something seems off.

The nightmares are back and this time she doesn't want them fixed. They're telling her something. Just what, she can't say, but it's as if a piece of her is being stolen. The content changes, but the themes are the same—her heart ripped from her chest, brain matter spooled from her ears, unknown hands peeling back the fine layers of her skin—each nightmare more unnerving than the next, stealing her breath as she wakes.

Returning to Benjamin for a re-tweak might make Gill happy, but where were her needs and wants in that? *He knows I hate going there!*

"I'm catching a sky-shuttle down to the Snowys this morning," Gill reminds her at breakfast. She's made pancakes with Davidson's plum jam, as expected. "Try to get a shot of a Mountain Pygmy-possum."

Lauren nods and sips her coffee. Gill's away a lot, forever searching for some elusive creature, and she gets lonely. He's often gone for weeks, and it's tough with no-one to talk to.

"I might head off to the Daintree Painters Exhibition then," says Lauren, and Gill snorts.

"Thought you'd be sick of seeing amateurs strut their stuff."

"Hardly."

If she could change one thing about her husband, it'd be the elitist air he conveys. Though no relationship's perfect, and he does have his good points. It's just that lately, his less desirable traits needle more than usual. Maybe time apart will do them good. It certainly won't harm.

As he drives off, his last words hang in the humid air—a threat to take her to Benjamin upon his return—and she closes the front door, then heads to her studio to paint.

***

A few hours in, she runs out of turpentine, and drives into town to replenish.

"Painting your house, are ya?" The customer standing next to her at the hardware store wears paint-splattered overalls, red-rimmed glasses and combat boots. A green bandana corrals her mass of curly red hair.

"No, a canvas," Lauren replies. "I'm an oil painter."

"No shit? Me too!" Her grin is broad and uncensored; Lauren can't help but return it. "Tracey Black-Allsopp," she says, extending a hand to shake. "And you are?"

"Lauren Spurling. Are you exhibiting with the Daintree Painters?"

Tracey blows out a loud raspberry, scrunching her nose. "Nuh! Don't go in for clubs and committees. Not my scene. People jostling for importance, strutting around like royalty. I prefer to do my own thing."

Lauren smiles and surprises herself. "Want to grab a coffee?" She rarely acts

out of spontaneity these days, but she's taken in by the woman's confidence and refreshing honesty.

"Why not?" says Tracey. "But screw the coffee." She lifts her bottle of turpentine. "Let's get on the turps."

"Huh?"

"Go get us a *real* drink. I could kill a G & T right now." Lauren checks her watch. It's shy on midday. "Oh, come awwwwn," pushes Tracey. "Day drinking's the best kind there is."

Lauren smiles. Not much of a drinker— her epilepsy put paid to that—she nevertheless agrees, mesmerised by her exotic find.

At Mietta's Bar and Grill, they have a drink and share a vegetarian pizza. Then, after discovering how close they live to each other, Tracey grabs a bottle of wine and insists on continuing the chat back at her place.

"You'll have to excuse the mess," she says, as they walk through the front door. "Jace is away at work. He's a truckie, or a self-drive observer they're called nowadays." She makes air quotations, then rolls her eyes. "I prefer truckie. It's sexier, don't you think?" She winks and clicks her tongue. "Anyway, there's no way I'm picking up the kids' crap over and over, only to have them throw it out again. It's a game, I swear, a game called, 'Let's Piss Mum Off'."

"You've got kids?" asks Lauren. She glances around the cluttered living room, taking in toys, books and art supplies. It's a galaxy apart from her own living room; she might as well be on Mars.

"Two rug rats. A pigeon pair. Briar's ten and Miles is twelve. And you…?"

Lauren shakes her head, but can't bring herself to say she never wanted any. She's not sure why. Tracey doesn't seem the type to take offence. But the words won't leave her lips. So, she changes the subject. "How'd you end up in the Daintree?"

With a glass of wine each, the two women sink into the soft cushiony sofa, riddled with dog hair, and Tracey tells Lauren her story. She was once a police officer in Sydney and had planned an around Australia road-trip with her workmate, Cadie.

"Close on twenty years ago now." She shakes her head in disbelief. "Back in the petrol days. Time flies though, hey?" After taking a sip of her wine, she continues, "Anyhow, we crossed paths with Jace hauling refrigerated goods in his truck. He drove the big diesel rigs back then. Almost seemed to tail each other, meeting up at rest stops at the end of each day." She snorts. "At first, he had eyes for Cadie. She's gorgeous, Cadie-Coo, but talk about waiting on a rocking horse to shit! She doesn't even *like* men." She leans back and laughs, and it comes from her belly, deep and sonorous.

Have I ever laughed like that? Wonders Lauren. *So free. So unreserved?*

"Then *I* got a look in." She gives Lauren a suggestive eyebrow raise. "Once you try a little Tracey Black, you ain't never goin' back." It's cringe-worthy but Lauren laughs, nevertheless. "Anyhow, we kept talking when I returned to Sydney, a long-distance kind of thing, because Jace lived up here in the Daintree, and before long it was crunch time. Make or break. And voilà." She gestures with a flourish. "What about you? What's *your* story?" Lauren hesitates, not sure where to start, and Tracey says, "Have you always lived around here?"

"Um…no…"

"So, where'd you grow up?"

"Aah…" Struggling for words, she sees fields of wheat and a farmhouse, a woman and a man, and two other girls, but there are no names, no clear faces. The details are blurry, like reaching for a cloud, trying to grasp it in your hand, only to watch it break apart and wisp away. The awkward moment lengthens, Tracey staring and waiting for her to speak, until two children burst through the front door, carrying schoolbags and yelling. Lauren gasps at the bustle and sonic assault, and hides her relief.

"Give it to me!" screams the girl, thrusting a hand out.

"Nup," taunts the boy.

"Muuum! Miles has my holo-watch and won't give it back."

"Miles," warns Tracey.

"I'm just trying to show her how to use it."

"Give it back to Briar," Tracey orders. She says it in a deadpan tone as though this kind of thing is a common occurrence.

Miles holds the watch above his head and Briar jumps to reach for it. After a moment, Tracey huffs, gets up from the sofa and grabs it from her son's hand, giving him a gentle cuff across the back of the head.

"Oi! Muum!"

"Here." She hands the watch to Briar. "Now come meet a new friend. This is Lauren." She turns to check. "Okay if we call you Loz?"

A flush of warmth runs through Lauren, the nickname making her feel special. Though she can only imagine what Gill might say. 'Loz?' His face twisting into a contemptible sneer. *'Why didn't you insist on them calling you Lauren, for Christ's sake?'*

Briar sidles up to show Lauren her watch, bringing warmth and the sweet smell of strawberries. For a split second, Lauren sees a bloodied hand; it grips a pulsating heart, the image flashing through her brain. She flinches and puts a hand to her chest, struggling to refocus.

Briar says, "I got this yesterday for my birthday." She switches on a hologram. The image flickers as the girl spins and twirls on the face of the watch. "Come on, Loz," says Briar. "Come dance." Briar pulls Lauren from the sofa as music pumps through the in-room speakers and the hologram projects on the wall.

Tracey jumps to her feet to join them, employing overly enthusiastic, out-of-date dance moves and Lauren laughs, pushing the awful image of the bloodied hand and heart away. She jumps about, following the girl's moves, trying to keep up. Meanwhile, Miles rolls his eyes and slumps off down the hall, muttering under his breath.

"Not cool enough for ya, mate?" Tracey calls after him.

When the music stops, Tracey tells Briar to do her homework and then takes Lauren by the hand, leading her to the backyard studio.

"Come see my work," she says.

Inside the small shed, Lauren flips through canvasses, marvelling at the vibrancy of colour and off-kilter compositions. The faces and bodies of the human figures are grotesque, yet beautiful, the style naïve but also somewhat sophisticated. It's Tracey on canvas, unadulterated. Unashamed. Her own work seems constrained and dull by comparison.

"Stay for dinner?" Tracey asks when the tour is over.

"Thanks," says Lauren. "But I'd better get going."

"Didn't you say your husband's away?" Lauren nods and her new friend grabs her by the hand. "Then I won't take no for an answer. Who wants to go home to an empty house?"

***

When Lauren finally arrives home, she flops onto the black leather lounge and tries to unscramble her thoughts. It's like eating green apples your entire life, only to be presented with a plate of mangoes, lychees and cherries. Her palate has come alive, bursting with colour, flavour and texture. She'd had a wonderful time at Tracey's, so much so that it's left her with an aftershock, something primeval bubbling within.

What have I closed myself off from, by not having kids?

Gill wouldn't approve of her new friend. He'd hate her on sight, hate everything about her, especially the qualities Lauren admires the most—her vivacity and boisterous, brutal honesty. He'd hate the lot, the entire unapologetic mess. He'd call her shrill, loud, vulgar. But then, Lauren doesn't always enjoy the company of *his* friends either, especially not his best friend from school, her neurologist Dr Benjamin King. She tolerates him, for Gill's sake— puts up with his arrogance and tiresome lectures, and the bored, dismissive look he gives her whenever she offers an opinion— because that's what you do when you're married. Even so, Gill would be nothing but disparaging about Tracey. She'd bet money on it.

When he arrives home, Lauren's proven

right. They bump into Tracey at the supermarket and on the drive home, Gill says, "Oh my God, what was *that*?" Lauren doesn't bother to reply but when he leaves two weeks later, off to the Northern Territory to find a Black-flanked Rock-wallaby, she invites Tracey over. It's a tad childish, this mini-rebellion, but she's exhilarated by it, nonetheless. It's not as though Gill would ban her from seeing Tracey—he's not a *complete* control freak—but he'd make his disapproval well known, and she doesn't want to deal with that right now.

Tracey accepts the invitation straight away. Jace is still on the road, and the kids are both on sleepovers, so she's keen for company.

A little disappointed not to see Briar and Miles—Lauren had planned a film night with popcorn and pizza, lying on mattresses, blankets and pillows set in front of the wall-screen—she makes gnocchi with burnt sage butter instead, and scopes out the wine cellar for vintage reds. An adult night in will do just as well.

"I could have a sleepover too!" suggests Tracey over the phone. Lauren hadn't offered—it feels a step too far—though it's crazy to even think like that. Tracey's a friend, nothing more. They aren't embarking on some clandestine affair or doing anything *that* untoward. Still, an overwhelming sense of betrayal swamps her, her every synapse flooding with guilt. But Benjamin stays when he comes up from Sydney. So, why not Tracey?

In the end, she agrees and makes up the spare room.

***

"This is amazing." Mouth full of gnocchi, Tracey points her fork at her bowl. "You

have to show me how to make this." She swirls the wine in her glass, then takes a sip. "So, tell me about you, Loz. What was life like before you met Gill?"

Lauren hesitates to answer, once more unable to find names and places, her thoughts and memories muddied.

"Well, I grew up on a farm," she eventually says. "Went to primary school, high school, you know, the usual sort of thing... Oh, I'd better check the dessert." She jumps up and heads to the kitchen, and when she returns, she manages to steer the conversation to somewhere more Tracey-centric.

After eating apple and cinnamon crème caramel cake, Tracey moans and stretches back on the leather lounge, plonking her socked feet on the Lalique crystal coffee table. Lauren stifles a wince, knowing Gill would be horrified.

"I might have to move in if this is how you cook every day!" Tracey announces.

Lauren tops up their wines, then settles into a recliner. They sip their drinks and listen to the sounds of the rainforest outside, the catbirds and whipbirds, the frogs and cicadas, then Tracey jumps up and grabs a photo from the mantel. "Your wedding photo!" She studies it, then looks sideways at Lauren. "Two hotties, huh?" Returning her focus to the image, she says, "Look how *young* you both are."

"Eighteen," admits Lauren, a flush warming her face. Is she embarrassed, or is it the wine? "We met in high school."

"High school sweethearts, hey?" Tracey smiles and puts the photo back on the mantel. "I love old photos. Got any more?"

Lauren nods, then flicks on the wall-screen and scrolls through to her image file.

"Oh, can I?" asks Tracey. She takes over the scrolling, swiping right to left to watch the story of Gill and Lauren unfold. They're on-screen, young and fresh-faced, dressed up for the formal, out on nature hikes, on holiday, floating in the Mediterranean, enjoying an anniversary dinner in Paris, strolling the streets of Venice.

"They're all of you and Gill," Tracey notes. "No photos of your family?"

"Oh. No. They were lost."

"What do you mean lost?"

"Wiped from the cloud by mistake. It was so devastating, like losing everything in a house fire."

"Right," says Tracey. She stares at Lauren for a long moment, then frowns. "But you didn't lose the photos of you and Gill?"

"No…" Lauren pauses to think. "I… guess they were in a different folder." Tracey has a strange look on her face and who can blame her? Why has she never asked Gill about this? She'd simply accepted his explanation. But how could there be so many photos of them and none of their families? She feels like a fool for not questioning it.

"Wanna see some of mine?" says Tracey and she casts her family photos from her phone to the screen. Lauren's glad for the distraction, some light relief from the needling of her thoughts.

"And this is Briar's fifth birthday party," says Tracey, continuing to scroll.

Lauren nods and smiles at the gap-toothed grin of little Briar. So sweet and angelic. And there's Miles as a baby, playing in the bath, cuter than cute. She sighs, and a physical reaction rolls through her body, hitting with the force of a tsunami; her heart aches with something she can't quite grip onto and her thoughts tumble in the swirling wash. Is this… longing? The bloodied hand and beating heart is there again, papered on a billboard in her brain.

Tracey glances over. "Are you okay?"

"Yes… I'm fine," says Lauren, forcing a smile. "Just tired."

Tracey turns off her phone and the photos stop casting. She puts a hand to her forehead and moans. "You know what? I think I've got a migraine coming on."

"A migraine? Oh, you poor thing."

"Yeah, they're cluster headaches. It's like someone drilling into your forehead, above your eye."

"I'll get you some painkillers." Lauren jumps up and heads to the kitchen, returning with two tablets and a glass of water.

"Thanks," says Tracey.

Lauren grimaces to see her friend in pain. "You know, maybe you should see my neurologist," she suggests. "He's done wonders for my epilepsy."

***

In bed, Lauren tosses and turns, trying to figure things out. Deep truths she's always believed are thrown into question. Was it a joint decision for her and Gill not to have children? Or Gill's alone? The longing borne out of watching Tracey's family photos floods her, coursing through body and brain, and pooling in the chambers of her heart. She *does* want kids. Maybe always has. But how could she have convinced herself otherwise?

And where are her family? Why has she never heard from them? Asked after them? Thought about them? Until now, until becoming friends with Tracey. Her head's clouded, draped with sticky cobwebs. She reaches for memory—an image of her childhood home, the faces of her parents—only to get caught up and cocooned.

***

When Gill returns home from his trip a week later, Lauren hits him with a barrage of questions. He's settled into the lounge, glass of single malt whisky in hand.

"It's that Tracey woman, isn't it?" He strokes his throat while looking down his nose.

"What?"

"She's putting ideas in your head, trying to come between us."

"What? No! Why would you even think that?"

"I knew she wasn't good for you."

"This is *not* about Tracey," says Lauren. "This is about us, about me, about not being able to remember my family, for Christ's sake. What's going on with me, Gill?"

He twirls his drink; ice cubes clink against the glass. "You know my thoughts on the matter. You know what I'm going to say."

Lauren huffs, then heads out to her studio to lose herself in paint.

***

She gets a text from Tracey while in bed that night and shoots through a reply. The ting-ting of messages flying back and forth pulls an annoyed Gill from his novel. He bookmarks his page and frowns.

"Who's that?"

"Tracey."

"Oh... her." His distaste is unmistakeable but Lauren lets it go. "What does she want?"

"The number for Ben's surgery. She gets cluster headaches, so I recommended him."

"Really?" says Gill. He raises an eyebrow, then looks back down at his book. A slow smile grows on his face and Lauren frowns.

"What's so amusing?"

He sets the book on his bedside table and rubs his chin. "You have to admit, it's pretty rich that you'd recommend Ben to a friend when you won't even go see him yourself."

"I haven't had a seizure in years, Gill."

"Because of Benjamin."

"Yes... okay... because of Benjamin," mutters Lauren.

"But the nightmares are recurring and your memories are failing. You said so yourself."

"Yes, but..."

He turns to address her fully. "Just a quick check-up. That's all I ask. We could even combine it with a trip to your parents."

"Really?"

Gill shrugs. "Sure. Why not? It's been a while since we've seen them." He reaches across and wraps her in his arms. "But first a trip to Benjamin's surgery. You know how frightening your seizures can be. What if you had one while I'm away?" He kisses her on the forehead. "I just want what's best for you sweetheart, surely you can see that?" She relaxes into his embrace and her anxiety fades.

"Alright then, if it makes you happy, I'll go."

"Good." He extracts himself from her embrace and reaches for his phone. "I'll make the arrangements now."

***

The consultation is rescheduled twice, Gill getting a hot lead on a Silver-headed Antechinus sighted in South Australia, then another straight after about a Kangaroo Island Dunnart.

With Gill away for several weeks, and with no-one answering the door at Tracey's house, the loneliness hits Lauren more than usual. She tries to paint, but her focus has deserted her along with everybody else.

She calls around to Tracey's again, and is relieved to see signs of life this time, toys scattered about the front yard. She brings a bottle of wine and home-made rice-paper rolls. The kids will be at school, so they'll be able to catch up without interruption.

"Hey, you!" she says, when Tracey answers the door. "Where have you been?"

"Excuse me?" Tracey frowns at her as though she's some kind of lunatic.

Lauren raises the wine and container of food. "I brought refreshments. Day drinking's the best kind, I hear."

Tracey keeps staring at her strangely and says, "I'm sorry, but you've obviously got me confused with somebody else." She goes to close the door and Lauren shoves her booted foot in to hold it ajar.

"Do you mind!"

"What the hell are you playing at Trace?" says Lauren. "It's me, Loz."

Tracey huffs and opens the door wide. Planting her hands on her hips, she fixes Lauren with an awful snarl. "Listen here, lady. I don't know who you think you are, or how you've come to know my name, but if you don't get your fucking foot out of my door, I'll ring the police."

Lauren gasps and steps back. "But... I don't understand."

"Psycho," mutters Tracey as she slams the door.

***

When Gill arrives home that afternoon, Lauren tells him about her strange interaction with Tracey.

"What'd you expect?" he says, with a shrug. "I warned you about toxic people like her. She's probably jealous of you, jealous of your art."

Lauren frowns and shakes her head. "No, I don't think it's that."

"Well, what else would it be?"

She rubs her forehead and sighs. "I don't know. I really don't know."

"Just forget about her," says Gill. "You don't need people like that in your life."

Lauren nods and purses her lips. "Yeah, maybe you're right."

Gill smiles wide. "I'm always right, darling. You should know that by now."

***

"The last remodel may have affected her recognition memory," Dr Benjamin King says, tapping the end of a pen against his thin lips. He sits opposite Lauren and Gill, addressing his commentary to her husband. Lauren might as well be a sick puppy brought to a veterinarian.

"Is that even possible?" Gill pinches the skin at his throat and frowns.

"Oh yes," says Benjamin, punctuating his words with a decisive nod. "It's quite common, I'm afraid. Neuro-remodelling can cause unwanted alterations to certain areas of the brain, but it's reversible, an easy fix." He turns to acknowledge Lauren for the first time. "Sounds as though we've affected the function of your hippocampus, but we'll have those memories flooding back soon enough, don't worry." His smile is stiff, perfunctory, and Lauren nods to reply. "Why don't you head to the neuro-room. I'll be along soon."

She does as he asks, making her way

down the corridor.

In the cold, sterile treatment room, she climbs into the lay-back chair, knowing the drill. She's been here before, many times. Reaching a hand around to the base of her skull, she feels under her hairline where the neuro-shunt was inserted all those years ago. Benjamin will be in soon to remodel her neurons and synapses, fix faulty connections and obsessive thought patterns, clear her recurring nightmares. She's always had a tricky brain, one prone to anxiety and depression, and had developed epilepsy in her mid-twenties, her seizures uncontrolled by medication alone. It's a necessary evil coming here, but she can't help the jolting physical reaction that surfaces whenever she sits in this treatment chair. She glances around the room in search of a vomit-bag, just in case.

As she waits, her leg jiggles and her heart races. One too many coffees on-board, she gets up, scooting back down the corridor to the toilets opposite Benjamin's office.

Drying her hands with paper towel, she pauses. Gill and Benjamin are outside in the corridor, speaking in hushed tones.

"Thanks for getting Tracey out of the picture, but it looks like we're still gonna need a re-tweak. Lauren's asking about her family and bringing up the kids issue again."

"Right," says Benjamin. "We'll give it another go, but if it keeps recurring we might have to consider surgery."

"Isn't that dangerous?"

"Well… it's a risk versus benefit thing."

What? Surgery! Lauren steps out into the corridor, right into the middle of their conversation. "Gill?" She stares at him and then at Benjamin. "What the hell's going on? What was that about Tracey?"

Gill blanches, then turns to look at Benjamin. He nods and the two men launch, each grabbing an arm.

"Hey, stop!" screams Lauren. "Let go!"

They drag her down the corridor towards the neuro-room as she struggles, kicks and yells.

"Help! Someone please help! They're screwing with my brain!"

"It's okay," Benjamin calls out to the staff who've poked their heads around the corner. "She's suffering a psychotic episode. I've got it all in hand. Go back to what you're doing."

Gill and Benjamin frogmarch Lauren to the neuro-room, and her husband—the man who's *supposed* to love, honour and protect her—throws her into the chair and straps her in.

"Don't do this, Gill!" she pleads, still thrashing about.

"Oh, *quit it*, Lauren! Sit still!" He holds her head against the headrest while Benjamin secures a strap across her forehead. "It's for the best. You're much better when you've had your treatment. Far more compliant and settled within yourself. It's better for everyone all round."

"How can you say that?" hisses Lauren. "How can this possibly be better for me?" Thick straps are fastened at her wrists and ankles; she bucks and writhes against the tight hold.

"You'll see," says Gill. "This happens every time. You always put up a protest, but only I know what's good for you, what's good for us. Just trust me on that."

"Did I ever even *have* epilepsy, Gill?" she whispers, tears spilling onto her cheeks.

"Well…" He shrugs. "You *did* have a seizure once." He glances across at Benjamin and snorts. "Brought on by a cocktail of stimulants and psychoactive meds, of course. I mean, how else was I going to get you here?" She screams and spits at him. He wipes it away with the sleeve of his shirt, then stuffs a gag in her mouth, securing it with another strap. "She's all yours, Kingy," he says, stepping back. "And go ahead with the surgery. It'll save us from having to return."

"Diagnostics first," says Benjamin. Through the opening in the back of the headrest, he inserts a lengthy probe into the neuro-shunt at the base of Lauren's skull. She screams and sobs while he taps on the keyboard, delivering red hot pain that sends her body into convulsions.

"Yep, that's where we need to be. Just... there." He taps some more on the keyboard, then removes the probe. Her tensed body slumps and she sucks in air through her nose. The tight gag muffles her screams as Benjamin darts a needle into her thigh. The room spins, and her eyelids grow heavy.

No! Please God, no!

Benjamin picks up a scalpel, and as the dark closes in, Gill smiles and gives her a wave.

"See you on the flip side, sweetheart. Night night."

RESTLESS
BY D.I. RUSSELL

The world is full of thinkers, congregated in spirit come the early hours. The *tick-tick-tick* of the minute hand stretches the night, an insomniac's nightmare, if you'll excuse the oxymoron. Here I sit by the kitchen window, warming my aching fingers around a steaming, strong black coffee. I watch the stars blink out one by one; clouds oozing across the sky as ink through a blotter. A rumble of thunder, distant for now.

Still the bulb in the lamp flickers in response. Temperamental old house! Never liked the storms, just like my dear Josephine. A flashlight and candles would be readied at the slightest hint of a storm. I can still name every plate in the human skull, but can't remember where we keep the matches. She could always find them.

I glance out of the window.

It's awake out there, not that it ever sleeps.

I abandon my vigil to run a finger along the dusty titles on my shelves. While the hunter has his trophies and the lover his conquests, I have my books. A marking of Academia. A record of thought.

I'm dwelling on the thinkers again. Stupid old man.

Hungry for distraction, I slide out a volume on the endocrine system. That should take my mind off things.

The moment I return to my station, lightning splinters the bleak horizon. Pushing my face against the window, my breath fogs the cold glass. I wipe the condensation away, staring into the darkness.

Josephine's garden, her pride and joy, now left to the weeds. The vines and grass grow rampant, a spreading ivy tumour. If a soul is destined to find its mate, then why not its resting place? Her place was out there, surrounded by beauty. Life nurtured by her own fragile hand.

We never had children.

Sometimes I think about Josephine drifting through the garden, tracing her fingers through the now waist-high grass, shaking her head. Sometimes she cries. Sometimes she cries for me.

Still, she never goes near that patch where the weeds refuse to grow; the patch of pale-clay soil no rain will darken; the patch that stinks of formaldehyde when the wind blows towards the house.

These are the things I dwell on, alone and cold, in a house that doesn't like the storms.

Speaking of which, here's the thunder.

It was Josephine's idea to bury the damn thing out there. An awkward present from my colleagues at the university. More fitting than a watch or bottle of aged Scotch, they said. Would be an interesting anecdote for all those boring medical seminars, they said. Plucked straight from a corpse that day, they *implied*.

In hindsight the Scotch would have been a preferred farewell gift. A nip or two of glorious burning sedative. Coats my stimulated neurones with a fatty layer. Interferes with my body's signals that fire like the guns of war: never sleeping.

The first drops of rain start to fall, and I listen to the patter on the roof. Some find this soothing, yet I've never succumbed to sleep by this lullaby.

I sip from my cup.

Lightning. The flash reveals the garden, the dead grass. Even through the bitter tang of the coffee and the ozone freshness of the storm, I smell the faint sweetness of acetone.

I have no fear it will claw through the soil and come lurching in the rain. It sits in a suspension the colour of urine, creamy slime hanging through like spiderwebs, encased in smooth, flawless glass. An interesting anecdote indeed.

I sigh and open my book. Three hours to dawn. I have to stop *thinking*.

It's worse at night. As the day slips into silence and the sun slinks to the horizon, you try and snatch some rest in your empty bed. All you find are the cracks in the ceiling, and the ticking of that infernal clock. It records the seconds of suffering like a devil counting souls.

And in the dead of night, in those silent, lonely hours…I can feel it *thinking*.

I wonder what it ponders, out there, all alone, soaking in chemicals in the dark womb of the ground.

Which poor bastard ended up on the university slab that day, to be hacked and separated? Is this why it won't rest?

So, it lies in my Jospehine's beloved garden. It thinks and schemes.

What does it ruminate as the worms squirm past; grotesque, plump bodies squashed against the glass?

Another distant rumble of thunder. The continuous cadence of rain on the roof. I shiver.

We are not that different. It has the grave; I have the house. We never sleep. We live in the dark. We exist alone.

Josephine.

The world is full of thinkers.

Only three hours to dawn.

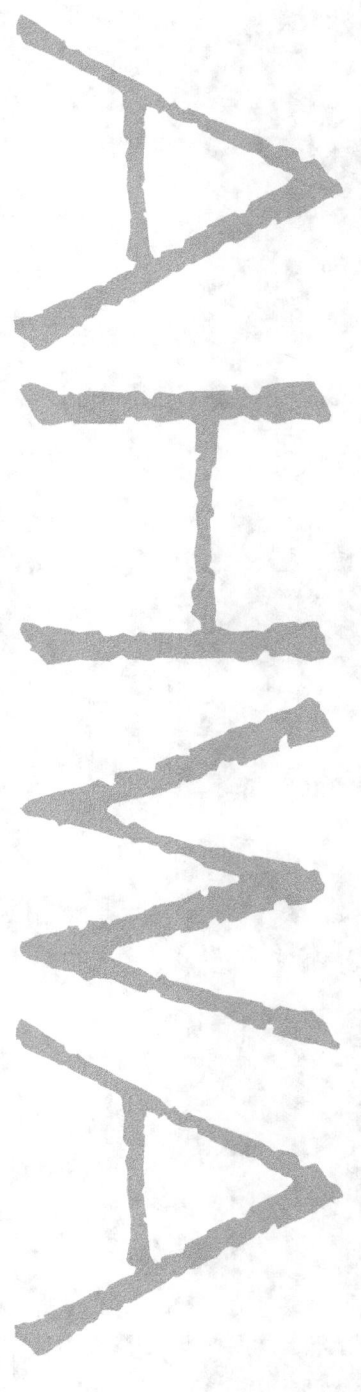

THE FRUITS OF LABOUR
BY MARK TOWSE

The house became mine on 12th December 1978, well over a decade ago. I'd just come out of a marriage that lasted longer than it should, a lot less affluent but a damn sight happier. I wanted to move on, and as a city dweller all my life, the country seemed like the perfect place to reset, to breathe new life into my writing career.

Climbing mountains, playing in old castle ruins, and telling ghost stories while surrounded by fog are just some of the treasured memories from family holidays long ago. I wanted that air of mystery back, to channel my inner kid. Not so much a whim, more a compulsion. As soon as I rolled up the driveway to the third house on my list—Sanctuary Place—the hairs on my neck bristled. I felt it as my fingers coiled around the door handle, too, childlike awe that sent a shudder of giddiness down my spine.

My search was finally over.

You've heard the tale before, the too good to be true price, the nearby cemetery, the rumours around town, all the warnings of classic horror, but when you're smitten, it's hard to see through the mist. Hell, those factors likely only made me want it more at the time.

Even mother approved of its stateliness, only diluting her enthusiasm with thoughts of it being "far too big for a single man." Bitterness towards the end of my marriage with Denise was something she carried around for quite some time. "People give up too easily these days."

The weather was abhorrent the day I collected the keys. At least that's how I recall it. I suspect memory often adds layers of desolation to winter seasons gone. Roads were gritted, but the snow was winning, especially on the country ones. I took it slowly, but it only added to the anticipation, and by the time I rolled up the driveway, gravel crunching underneath the soft white coating, I could hardly contain myself. Songs crackled from the radio as I sat in the warmth of the car, admiring my new home. I could have stayed there for hours, taking it all in. Weathered but proud, vibrant green ivy wrapping around crumbling golden stone and grounds filled with various songbirds.

Everything about it was grand, outside and in. Double doors opened to a magnificently ornate staircase that split the house in two. Impressive but dusty cobweb-covered chandeliers conjured scenes of music and laughter. But its sheer size also induced a feeling of inexplicable sadness, as though the good times had been and gone.

I wanted to resuscitate it, give it meaning again.

Before arranging for the removal van, I often drove down just to familiarise myself with the house and its surroundings. I spent hours just mulling around the place, inspecting its bare bones, looking for secret doors or shifting walls. Did I mention I was a writer? Etched into the corner of the main dining room floor, I found a heart, the initials *MT, KT,* and *ET* scratched out in its centre.

In the middle of the countryside, buried

between sloping hills, the nearest house at least half a mile away, the property was quiet and serene. Perfect, in other words. The orchard in the expansive backyard would give me the most pleasure and soon become a second obsession.

The back bedroom became my study, and I filled it with books and furnishings to make it as comfy as possible. Overlooking the then skeletal fruit trees that subtly turned to rolling hills, marked off only by a rusty collapsed wire fence, it was the perfect place to write. Even though I could see my breath, I was already picturing the blossom and could almost taste the perfumes wafting through the open sash window. Denise would have said I was stark raving mad, but she was out of my life, and my time was my own.

The first couple of weeks went by quickly, days taken up by painting endless walls, attempting to fix things with my limited knowledge, and sitting in front of my typewriter. The moans from the old pipes, the creaks from the walls, and the trespassing wind that whistled its haunting tune were yet to inspire, but I knew it was only a matter of time.

The first spring arrived bang on schedule, transforming my *backyard* into a wonderland of colour almost overnight. No words came, but plenty of fruit did over the coming months, a bounty of ripe apples, pears, plums, and peaches, to name just a few. Best fruit ever. Perfection. Only two trees failed to provide anything but leaves, and they stood side by side at the edge of the dam, looking sad and out of place.

Friends from all locations flocked to Sanctuary Place in those first few months. Depending on the weather, you would find us in the main hall or courtyard area, drinking, singing, dancing, and laughing. I guess it was my way of trying to reignite the property's flame.

And then there was Frank, a friendly but stubborn oaf I'd known since boarding school. Constantly trying to matchmake, he would insist on his *current* date bringing a friend along. He never knew when to give up. I must admit I was tempted once—Nancy—an artist who gushed over the house as much as I first did.

One of many things I will live to regret.

Slowly but surely, the honeymoon period wore off, and by the time winter looped back around, the familiar feeling of disappointment was knotting in my chest. Friends had lost interest in making the long drive, and the orchard looked sad.

Blank pages taunted me.

The following spring, things would change. It was an unseasonably warm start, bringing premature blossom and an array of wildlife to the algae-stained fountain. Hope washed over me again, and although I'd written no words, they felt close.

Then one morning, I looked out the study window and somehow knew things would be different. Blossom had bloomed on the two trees near the dam, paling the other flowers into relative insignificance. Spectacular shades of red and pinks demanded attention, almost too vibrant to be real.

It was as if they were calling me.

That small patch of grass between the two trees soon became my new favourite spot. The view of the house, the tranquillity, the perfumes—it all had an energy about it, something the house didn't. And that's where the first few words spilled from the dusty catacombs of my mind onto paper.

The two trees soon started to bear fruit unlike any other. It was perfectly round with skin like a peach but paler and even more tender as though it could break at the slightest of knocks. I picked one, the ripest-looking piece, and held it to my nose. Such a fascinating scent. A cocktail of perfumes that induced contrasting melancholy and happiness, a feeling of wanting to laugh and cry simultaneously. Bursting with magnificent redness, it was all I could do not to gorge the fruit down immediately, but I made the experience last for as long as possible. Heart pounding, I rolled the fruit across my lips, inhaling its beauty, before finally sinking my teeth into its silky skin.

It burst with a popping sound, giving way to a heady sweetness that made my legs buckle. The treacly substance carried tangs of the ripest pomegranate, grape, pineapple, and more. Even the slightly bitter aftertaste was far from unpleasant. Each bite made me want it more. An unmistakable high went with it, too, an induced separation from the real world, unlike anything I'd experienced from the questionable substances Frank sometimes used to bring. Euphoric is the only way I can describe it.

They were the only two trees I netted; I let the birds have the rest.

Two thousand words found their way to paper that evening.

Time passed, and the fruit continued to ripen, becoming even larger, bursting with even more colour. And then something began to happen. I noticed a change. The fruit was still heavenly, intoxicating, but the roundness was undoubtedly developing into more of a pear-like shape.

My manuscript was at twenty thousand words and was my best work to date.

The next day, I turned up with my basket to find the slightly narrower half of the fruit had developed two small bumps adjacent to each other. I'm not talking about a single piece; I mean all of them, identically so. Something else, too. There was a series of small but unmistakable wrinkles where the two now distinct-looking shapes joined, like a—neck.

As I stuffed my face with piece after piece, I remember giggling but also feeling some disquiet. The bitter aftertaste was getting stronger, but so was my need for that sweetness.

Words flowed.

Excitement for my next bestseller was undeniable, and the following day, I couldn't get out of bed quickly enough. Morning sun poured through my open window like honey as I walked and stretched towards it, eager for a dose of nature's smelling salts. Squinting into the brightness, I surveyed my orchard with considerable pride. And even as my eyes fell on the two trees, impossibly full of fruit once more, I took it only as a good omen—that the house and grounds were coming alive again, bursting with creativity and hope.

A third bump appeared, slightly larger, like a nose, and below it, a crease resembling a smile. That morning, I got through four pieces and returned to my study to write six thousand words before lunch.

As fast as I could eat the fruit, it was growing back. What looked to be ears next, two bumps on the outer edge of the upper half. The fruit was undoubtedly getting bigger and heavier, but still, the branches refused to let it fall to the ground.

The following day, four stubs appeared, which, by dusk, had all matured into lengths passable as short limbs, albeit missing the hands and feet.

I needed more and more each day to sustain the high. I couldn't get the juice down my throat quickly enough. Five thousand more words found their way onto paper. Putting it down to arboreal aberrations, I denied what was happening, but each day the trees bore new fruit, and each time, the resemblance to a human baby became harder to pin on mother nature alone.

Fingers and toes appeared shortly after.

The metallic aftertaste got stronger every day, bringing back memories of scraped knees and disinfectant. It didn't stop me gorging, though, not wanting to waste a drop of that opulent redness.

I spent days in a haze, alternating my time between sitting behind the typewriter and refilling my creative juices under the tree.

Sixty thousand words and I was up to the final chapters.

The wail woke me up at 2.06 am, a muffled screaming that dragged me to the study window. I could see movement in the trees adjacent to the dam, and even before I had my dressing gown on, I knew what I'd find.

As I approached the treeline, eyes on the crying sexless babies, arching branches attached to their midriff like umbilical cords, I remember wondering if the moon had ever seen anything like it. As with their appearance, the noise they created was identical, high-pitched and deafening, just as nature intended. But their boneless limbs flailed in a way that would make even the Devil blush.

My stomach growled regardless as I observed their movements. It was just fruit, I justified, a deviant of mother nature. Ears ringing with their unbearable screeching, I picked the first one from the tree and sank my teeth into the neck, ripping the head away in a violent spray of red. One after the other, I stuffed my mouth with their juicy boneless flesh, draining their sweetness, basking in the innocence of the moonlight. I was insatiable. The taste was even sweeter, a further improved blend of fruit, earth, and syrup, all with perfect acidity that made the tongue sing and the belly crave more.

And that familiar aftertaste, of course.

Finally, the tree was empty, and I retired to my bedroom to sleep soundly.

The following morning, the fruit had replenished. Yes, in its early stages, but I knew it would shortly be singing to me once again. I ran my tongue across my top lip in anticipation.

Another six thousand words that day. I had only two chapters to go.

2.06 am.

The chorus woke me, slightly louder, but with the same muffled cries as though through stitched lips. Even tucked so far away, middle of the countryside, I was afraid someone would hear. Naked as the day I was born, I rushed outside and started picking the toddlers from the tree, shoving their juice-filled limbs into my mouth in a ravenous frenzy of popping, tearing, and guzzling. Only when the tree was empty did I stagger back, belly full and eager for the sun to rise.

I slept like a baby, waking up just after nine. New fruit was already growing on the two trees by the dam.

Five thousand words. One chapter to go!

As I said, obsession is blinding, much like love. Reality takes the chair behind, patiently waiting for the front seat to become free again.

In the early hours of the following morning, and like clockwork, the chorus began. But this was different, more of a synchronised moan than a cry. I jumped out of bed, my belly offering a groan as I scrambled through the darkness towards the source, ignoring the chill that seeped through my bones. The fruit that hung from the tree resembled small children now—all identical, all sexless. I ate every one of them and was still hungry for more.

When I woke just after seven that morning, the bitter but pleasant aftertaste still lingered at the back of my throat. I almost skipped towards that study window where my typewriter sat, my skin prickling at the thought of finishing my second novel.

As I took in the rolling landscape, habitually cracking my fingers, I let out a garbled cry, my eyes drawn to the two naked trees by the dam. I didn't want to believe it; I wouldn't let myself believe it.

The trees were—bare.

With tears in my eyes and grumbles from my belly, I ran as fast as I could, only to find it true. "No!" I cried, crumpling between them in a heap. "No, please!" I clawed at the ground, pleading for them to offer their fruit just one more time.

I was so close to being done.

But days grew shorter and evenings colder. The book remained unfinished. I could hardly summon the energy to get out of bed, never mind thoughts of writing. I wasn't eating. The fruit from that tree had become my only sustenance, the only taste tolerable.

Time went by painfully and slowly. Autumn days also proved poor nourishment for the house. Cold draughts sneaked through decrepit frames, taking with it all remnants of residual energy, leaving only sadness once more. Even the birds grew quiet, their songs few and far between.

Occasionally, the telephone would ring, but I ignored it, staying under the covers, shaking, knowing it wasn't the cold causing such a violent physical reaction. I thought I was dying, rotting away like unwanted fruit. I'm not sure how many days went by before the knock on the door came, and Frank's distant but familiar gruff voice broke the deafening silence. "Thomas!"

"It's not locked," I said.

More knocking followed. "Are you in there, Thomas?"

I knew he wouldn't come all this way and just leave. It wasn't in his nature to give up. Finally, the door clicked, and I heard his footsteps thundering up the wooden staircase. "Thomas?"

"In here."

"Thank God, I was beginning to—"

I saw the change in his face immediately. Some things you can hide, get away with, but shock is like a sucker punch that takes your breath away.

"What the hell?" he said, rushing to the bed, deep caverns running along his forehead.

I hadn't seen my reflection for weeks but had run my fingers over my face and could trace too easily the shape of my skull. My arms, too, were scrawny, skin hanging from the bone. "I've not been well, Frank."

"I tried to ring, Thomas. My God, look at you."

"Nearly finished the book."

"Never mind the goddamn book—you need a doctor! Can you get up?"

"I don't know."

He helped me to my feet and all but dragged me out of the room to the top of the staircase. "When was the last time you ate?"

I couldn't remember.

"You look like death, my friend. I thought country air was supposed to be good for you?"

I forced a smile. "Does anyone know you're here?"

He shook his head. "You need to come back. People miss you."

"I think I'll be okay now, Frank."

"You sure?" He looked me up and down, sighed, and shook his head again. "I'll lead, you follow, just in case those sparrow's legs you're borrowing give up the game."

As soon as he walked in, I could smell it, hear it even, rushing around his body, hidden beneath the pale and overripe flesh. I knew the taste wouldn't compare to the freshness from the branch, but nerve endings tingled regardless at the prospect of feeding again.

He got one step down before I pushed with what remaining strength I had.

I remember him reaching out as though trying to grab an invisible bar. The fall was clunky, noisy, and quick. He let out a long moan at the bottom, his limbs twitching and jerking in a contorted heap.

My adrenaline surged, but using the banister, I forced myself to take things slowly. I kept thinking how tragic it would be to fall, especially being so close to finishing the book. I owed it to Frank for

his suffering to not be in vain. Dormant for weeks, my belly grumbled loudly and relentlessly as I approached him.

It was awakening, and so was I.

I crouched towards him, observing the fear and confusion in his eyes. The scent was mesmerising. Blood pounded in my ears as I lifted his arm and sank my teeth into his toughened skin, allowing the bitterness to spill. As though being reborn, I could feel my strength replenishing with every mouthful. Stubborn to the end, Frank took a hell of a long time to die.

That evening, I finished the book.

It sits here in my study drawer now, has for many years. So lost in the haze, I didn't even consider the possible implications of its release. It is, after all, more confession than fiction and may well raise unwanted attention.

The book will have its day.

Since then, I've written two novels, both well received and profitable enough to do some upkeep around the place.

Frank is out there—in the orchard—with the others.

Each spring, the trees near the dam provide their fruit, but when the colder days draw in once more, that's when I go hunting. I can smell it from miles away these days, even hear it pumping in my ears. And I'm good at it now, much less clumsy in my efforts.

Sometimes I visit the town pub, *The Fox and Hen*, just to blend in, pass off as normal. It was there that I recently met Richard Brannigan, an old professor from the Grammar School. Interesting chap with even more intriguing stories, including the one about Sanctuary Place. It turns out he was good friends with Michael Turner, the owner. Although born into money, Richard said Michael was salt of the earth, one of the nicest chaps you could hope to meet. His wife, Katherine, was just the same, so welcoming, not an ounce of malice in her. They often held soirees for the locals, partying until the early hours. "Everyone loved them," Richard told me.

The pair were obsessed with each other, wanting to extend their family. Michael confided in Richard they'd been trying for children for months, even chosen names. Elliot for a boy, Elizabeth for a girl. Alas, no matter what they tried, the gift of children evaded them.

"And then that awful event. Such a goddamn tragedy!"

It was a robbery gone wrong. Two of the locals who attended the previous week's shindig had decided Michael and Katherine's hospitality was not generous enough. They came back in the early hours, hyped up on cocaine. Broke into Sanctuary Place, but that wasn't the worst of it.

"Unfortunately, Michael woke up." Richard's hands shook as he told the tale, knocking back whisky after whisky. Michael and Katherine's bodies were set on fire, their charred remains found at the dam's edge. "Nobody deserved that, especially those two."

The house fell into the hands of Michael's brother, Dylan, who tried selling it, but nobody wanted to go anywhere near the place. People said it gave off negative energy—made the hairs bristle but in the wrong way. Over time, rumours faded, interest waned, and Dylan finally decided the time was right.

And that's where I came in.

Although my hunger is strong, I still have a heart, and thinking of the pain Michael and Katherine must have endured over the years, especially after only offering goodness to the world, certainly pulls at its strings. I have nothing but admiration for how they managed to grow through the hardened soil and stone, persevering through freezing cold winters and hot, dry summers, stubbornly refusing to give up on each other, even in death.

One could be mistaken for thinking only their love for each other kept them going from ashes in the soil to ultimate cross-pollination. But the fruit those trees bear, the children they could only spawn after death, well, they're bursting with bad blood for sure.

What happened to them, not to mention the years spent buried under soil, would be enough to turn anyone to vengeful hate.

Me?

I'm an off-season killer with a thirst for blood, a conduit that shares the Turner family home. Nothing compares to the freshness of the branch, but "Beggars can't be choosers," as Mother often says.

Last week, she came to visit. She still disapproves of my single status. "Not healthy spending so much time alone, Thomas. This house needs a family—it's so cold and empty."

"Yes, Mother," I replied.

"It's been over ten years since you and Denise split."

"Yes, Mother."

"I'm ready to be a grandma, and babies don't grow on trees."

THE HOUSE CONTRITION BUILT
BY REBECCA FRASER

I've tried to leave me many times,

Escape my past, escape the crimes

That linger in my guilt-torn heart—

Outrun my shame. A brand-new start.

But no matter how I shed my skin—

The purging of residual sin,

My demons flush out where I hide,

I'm brought back to where I reside—

A house of pain, where conscience bleeds

A haunted place of past misdeeds.

I've tried to leave year after year—

I think I'm free…then I appear.

FEARFUL SYMMETRY
BY STEPHEN DEDMAN

Sarah enjoys cooking, and while she doesn't make elaborate meals as often as she did before the kids moved out, our kitchen is still well-equipped and she keeps the knives as sharp as her surgical tools.

I look at the cordless electric knife, press the button and listen to it whine as I wonder where to begin.

***

"Where does it hurt?"

"Right now?" I replied. "It doesn't." It wasn't exactly a lie—Katz had been my G.P. since I'd moved in with Sarah, and I wasn't sure I could fool her—but what's the point of being a copywriter for this long if you can't shade the truth a little?

"So, it's intermittent, not constant. Noted. Where does it hurt when it *does* hurt?"

"Mostly here," I said, pointing to the spot just above my bottom rib.

"Sarah says it's also your right arm. She was worried you were having a heart attack."

"It wasn't. She realized that. And it passed."

"She said you said that sometimes you feel as though you're drowning."

"Poor choice of words. I've never drowned, so how would I know?"

"It's not like you to be careless with words, Paul."

"Oh, that's just my job. I don't work 24/7."

"Hmm," Katz replied. She sounded skeptical. "How are you sleeping?"

"Why don't you ask Sarah?"

"You sleep in separate beds."

"Yeah, well… we tried sleeping in the same bed again after the operation, but my restless leg kept waking both of us up. I actually sleep a bit better knowing I'm not keeping her awake, too. Her schedule is bad enough already."

Katz didn't disagree. "Take your shirt off."

"My heart is fine," I protested, though I obeyed.

"It's your breathing that's worrying me at present," she replied. She waited until I'd stripped to the waist, then said, "You know you pointed at your scar?"

"They took out nearly half my lung," I snapped. "I think I'm allowed to be a little short of breath."

"Are you smoking?"

"No! I quit completely after the operation. For good."

Katz looked me in the eye. "No vaping or any of that shit?"

"No! I don't even need the nicotine patches anymore."

"But you still feel the craving."

"I was a smoker for more than forty years." It was closer to fifty, despite Sarah nagging at me for half of them. "When I was a schoolkid, if you couldn't make the football team, that was about the best way to prove you weren't gay. It was as close as we got to being a religious school." The fact that I was left-handed made me even more suspect, at least as far as my teachers were concerned, and it's just as well nobody knew I liked writing poetry.

Katz didn't laugh. She took a stethoscope out from her desk drawer and listened to my heart (I didn't have to remind her it's in the wrong place, a fact I wished Sarah had never told the kids) and my breathing, then checked my blood pressure. She seemed to hesitate for a moment, then moved the cuff to my left arm and checked it again. "Odd," she muttered, almost inaudibly, then said, "How much sleep are you getting?"

"It varies."

"On average."

"I don't know. Five, six hours, maybe."

"I'll take it that's on the *good* nights," she grumped. "Your restless leg?"

"Usually."

"And pain."

"Yeah, sometimes."

"Your right arm and the right side of your chest."

"Sometimes all the way down to the leg, yes, but like you said, it's intermittent. It almost never worries me during the day – never when I'm at work."

"Have you considered retiring? Or at least cutting back to part time?"

"The money's too good."

"Sarah makes good money. You own your house, you've put both your kids through college already –"

"I have bills to pay. Medical bills. And like I just said, the pain never bothers me when I'm at work. Can I get dressed, now?" I could see the scar in the mirror, and it bothered me. I've never felt completely whole since I had that chunk of lung removed – and, to be honest, that comment about Sarah's income had hit a nerve. Sure, we were comfortable, and hell, with the kids gone, we could probably have moved to a smaller house. But if I cut back to part-time, I'd be making less than she did, and even though I'd helped put her through medical school and was reaping the benefits, I was brought up to believe

the man should be the breadwinner.

"Sure," said Katz. She was silent for a moment as she watched me put my shirt on and tie my tie, then said, "You're in pain now, aren't you? Your right arm?"

She must have seen me wince. Fuck. "A little, yeah. Forgive me if I don't enjoy our little chats as much as I used to, but since the operation, doctors freak me out a little."

"Even Sarah?"

"A bit," I admitted. "You know what surgeons are like. Their answer to anything is to remove it. If thy right eye offend thee, cut it out, and all that." I wasn't sure Katz was up on the New Testament, but she nodded slightly.

"I'm recommending some more tests," she said. "I don't think the cancer's spread, there's no sign that it has, but I want to make absolutely sure. Your insurance should cover nearly all of it. Are the painkillers working?"

"Yes, but they take a while to kick in, and I feel good for an hour or so, but then they wear off much too soon."

"Don't take them any more often than the prescription says—they can cause serious liver and kidney damage – and don't drink alcohol when you're taking them. Be careful making important decisions, because they can also cause overconfidence. I don't want to prescribe any more painkillers or sedatives until you see a neurologist—and maybe a counsellor."

"You think it's all in my head?"

"Not all, but maybe some. That part of your chest that you say hurts, shouldn't hurt. Have you heard of phantom pain?"

"I've heard the expression."

"People who've had limbs amputated

often say they still feel pain in a body part that they no longer have. Most doctors used to think it was psychological, but it's more likely that it's neurological, that the nerves that used to be connected to that body part still keep working even when there's no connection."

"Something like muscle memory?" I can still play the guitar when I want to come up with a jingle (I'm no Heifetz, but I get by). I'm better on a keyboard, but sometimes the guitar has more of the sound I want.

"Something like that." She put the stethoscope back in her drawer. "Get those tests done and see a specialist as soon as you can—and if you have to wait, come back to see me if you're still having pain or trouble sleeping, or next month in any case. Say hello to Sarah for me."

My legs worked fine as I walked back to the Porsche, but the right foot seemed a little heavy on the accelerator as I drove back to the office.

**

I looked at the notes that had been left on my desk and groaned, then picked them up between my thumb and fingernail and carried them into Chris's office. "Please tell me this is meant to be a joke."

Chris looked up from his laptop with an implausibly innocent expression. "It's what the client wanted. If you'd been at the meeting –"

"I was at the doctor's. After reading this, I may have to go back there. He actually wants to use video of the storming of the Capitol to sell *hamburgers?*"

"Legal's looking into it. If they find we can't use news footage, if it's sub judice or whatever the term is, the boss wants you to do a budget for faking it. We'll have to build sets and hire doubles for the last scene when they burst into the dining room and find the president with the table full of fast food, anyway. The president doesn't have to speak or look like anybody in particular, which will save money: they're just going to shoot the back of his head."

"Like Lincoln," I said automatically. My fingers must have twitched, because the notes fell to the floor. "How expensive will it have to be for him to decide not to do it?"

"I don't know. If it helps, he only wants to show this in red states. He wants another version to show in the cities, with news footage of people lining up to be vaxed or to vote Democrat, maybe. I told him you'd come up with something he'd like."

"Okay, but—Jesus, Chris, January sixth wasn't just a joke! This is like trying to advertise Kool-Aid with pictures of Jonestown, or fire insurance with video of Waco!"

Chris shrugged. "Last I checked, Jim Jones and David Koresh didn't have enough supporters left to make a serious demographic. On the other hand, school shootings are great at selling AR-15 copies. Besides, you know how much this account is worth to the agency, and it's not like he can claim his burgers are tastier or healthier or cheaper than the competition's, at least not convincingly, so he needs a gimmick and this is what he chose. Sure, it's divisive, but ours not to reason why, right?"

**

Sarah was watching some documentary about Matthew Brady and the Civil War when I returned home, but she switched it off when I walked into the room. It doesn't worry me, but she knows it's still a sore point for my parents: my mother's a Daughter of the Confederacy and was pissed when both of our kids turned out to be boys and have so far stayed that way. When we can't avoid a family reunion, we try not to discuss politics or religion, especially since Robert announced he was bisexual. But Sarah likes to relax by immersing herself in what she calls the humanities: history, the arts. I'd do the same, but words and images and music are part of my job, and who wants to bring that shit home at the end of the day? Before Robert was born, I tried to become interested in some science, but I gave that up after Sarah told me that economics wasn't actually a science and I'd get more accurate predictions from a psychic helpline or magic 8-ball. "What did the doctor say?" she asked as I sat beside her on the couch.

"You mean you haven't spoken to her yet?"

"Patient-doctor confidentiality. It doesn't mean I can't tell her when I'm worried about your health."

"She's ordered more tests, and wants me to see a shrink."

"Mm. It can't hurt."

"It might. I bet the tests will."

"You're in so much pain already that it's almost certainly worth it."

"The pain comes and goes," I said. "I'm feeling fine right now. What say we go to your room after dinner, and I'll show you."

"Are you sure you're up to it?"

"They cut out part of one lung, not either of my balls," I said, more harshly than I'd intended.

"Well, I guess I could give you a physical," she said, batting her eyelashes. "But dinner first, okay?"

Maybe the sex would have been better if she'd sounded more encouraging, or if I hadn't nearly lost my temper, but I couldn't make her come and after I developed a cramp in my side and my leg, no position worked for me either. After we lay there a while, I kissed her and returned to my own room across the hall, trying not to limp too visibly.

A moment later, I heard music coming from behind her door: 'Try a Little Tenderness'. I was wondering whether that was intended as a suggestion or criticism, until I realized that she was re-watching *Dr. Strangelove*. I used to share her enthusiasm for the movie, but maybe I've seen it too often, because I really didn't feel up to watching it again. Instead, I tried playing the guitar for a while, hoping that would relax me, but my fingering was off, as though my left hand didn't know what my right hand was doing. Frustrated, I reached for the remote for my own TV and channel-hopped through the sports channels until I found something suitably mindless, not really caring who was playing or even what the game was, just as long as it was one side trying to beat the other. After about an hour, I changed into my pajamas, cleaned my teeth, and tried to sleep.

The pain woke me a few hours later, and after trying to ignore it, I called for Sarah.

***

"Your wife was right. It's not appendicitis, and I'm not going to suggest removing your appendix unnecessarily," Dr Katz reassured me, the next day. "She's probably right about it being a kidney stone, too, but that will –"

"Need more tests?"

She smiled evilly. "'Fraid so. But at least treating it shouldn't require surgery. If need be, we can break up kidney stones with ultrasound so they hurt less when you pass them. In the meantime, I'd suggest you watch your diet: cut down on salt, and at the risk of sounding like my grandmother, no bacon. And I'd give serious thought to taking a break from your job until you're better."

I groaned. "You're older than I am, and you haven't retired."

"I *like* my job, and this is not a good time for doctors to be quitting. But I don't take my job home with me or work every day; I have better things to do. It's called a work/life balance. But I'm not the one recovering from cancer. I'm in good shape for my age, but when I'm sick or too tired to do my job without making mistakes, I stay home."

"I was worried you were going to say it was all in my head. Psychosomatic."

"No, though that may be aggravating it. It's perfectly normal for cancer survivors to become hypochondriacs for a while afterwards, worrying that anything a little out of the ordinary might be a symptom of the cancer making a comeback. It's not a problem—if anything, it's a useful survival mechanism. They may feel as though their bodies have betrayed them, so they're on the alert."

"It's worse than that," I said. "I feel as though there's a war going on in my body, *for* my body, one side against the other and the side that started it not even caring if they both die. I know that's not rational, but every day, it's easier to believe."

Katz was silent as she absorbed this. "I can't help you with that. I'm going to refer you to a psychiatrist I know who's had a lot of experience with cancer survivors and their anxieties. I suggest you make an appointment as soon as she has one available."

***

I looked at the card once I was safely out of the surgery, and put it in my wallet rather than yield to the temptation to throw it away. I felt that I'd had enough of talking to doctors for a while. Don't get me wrong, I'm not an anti-vaxer and even on my best day, I don't think I could come up with a pitch for homeopathy that would fool more than a homeopathic proportion of the population. And I wouldn't have married a doctor if I didn't respect them. But they do tend to think alike, to only see one side of a problem, and I felt I needed to talk to someone with a different point of view.

I drove to the office, though I knew my real work wouldn't begin until Chris and I met McGregor, one of our clients, for nine holes of golf before lunch. I don't take the game seriously, and I have no idea what my handicap would be, but I was playing competently enough until I teed off for the fifth hole and my leg spasmed and I misjudged my swing, sending the ball into the rough far to the right of the fairway—or as Chris said softly, "slightly to the left of Fox News." He had to say it quietly, because McGregor was wearing a MAGA cap and ran most of his ads on Fox, Newsmax and OAN.

"I'll see you on the green," I told McGregor as he climbed into the golf cart with his secretary/caddy/mistress. He nodded and chuckled, and they headed off. I waited until they'd gone before limping back to our own cart, resisting the urge to use my nine-iron as a walking stick.

"I know we have to lose," said Chris, "but he'll be happier if we don't make it obvious—are you okay?"

"Not exactly," I admitted. "Right leg's been playing up since I had that operation. My doctor thinks I should take some time off, maybe even retire."

"I think he's probably right," said Chris, heading for the driver's side of the cart. I was about to protest, but admitted to myself that if my leg twitched again, we might end up in the water hazard.

"I didn't expect you to take her side," I replied. "It doesn't mean I can't work."

"No, but you don't need the money, and it's not like there's any other reason to do it."

"Health insurance."

"You're not covered by your wife's plan?"

"Well, not for dental," I mumbled, then, more clearly, "You don't like the job either, and I don't hear you talking about quitting."

"You own your house, your kids have jobs, and your wife makes good money. I've got a mortgage and child support to pay, and the job doesn't seem to be killing me yet."

"It's not killing me."

"Half-killing, then." He stopped the cart, climbed out to whack his ball down towards the green, then said, "That burger ad isn't still bugging you, is it? Let's look for your ball."

I followed him into the rough, wishing it wasn't too soon to take my next dose of painkillers. "I don't know," I said. "It's mostly my health, but the ad—yeah, a bit." I looked down, and saw my ball nestled between the roots of a tree. "I think this may be an unplayable lie."

"Yeah, but if we only told the truth, we'd be lucky to get any clients at all and I'd probably have to get a second job delivering UberEats. In a Datsun." He was silent for a moment, as I contemplated what to do with the ball, then said, "And I know you're conflicted, but no-one's asking you to take his side—well, not permanently, anyway. Next week, we may be selling gender-neutral electric bikes or fair-trade vegan kombuchas. We're not the ones tearing the country apart, we just—"

"Feast on the corpse?"

"You really aren't okay, are you?"

"No," I admitted, and recounted my last session with Dr Katz. "Maybe she's right. Maybe I should see a psychiatrist."

"A psychiatrist?" he replied. "Sounds to me like you need an exorcist."

***

We played through to the ninth hole, and while my right side didn't let me down too badly again, McGregor was in a jovial mood and offered us some of his favorite Scotch, a 21-year-old single malt. I tried to beg off, saying that I needed to drive home, but he said that one glass wouldn't hurt and poured us each a double. Knowing he wouldn't accept the fact that I was on medication as an excuse and that the account depended on making him happy, I sipped at it slowly and carefully while we tried to come up with a new gimmick to sell a men's bodyspray that smelled like a locker room that a pig had pissed in. My arm began to hurt after a few minutes, but at least it didn't cause me to spill the booze.

It was starting to get dark when I finally got out of there. My painkillers had worn off, but I figured it would be safe to take another one at about the time I arrived home. My leg hurt like hell, but apart from that it seemed to be doing what I needed it to—until a massive pickup ahead of me with a QAnon decal stopped abruptly and my foot stayed on the accelerator rather than moving to the brake. Unable to stop in time, I swerved into the left-hand lane hoping there wouldn't be another car coming. I downshifted as quickly as I could as the Porsche mounted the curb and drove onto someone's front lawn, then reached for the parking brake. The dog that had been running across the street, causing the truck to come to a sudden halt, looked at me stupidly, then began barking its fool head off. The pickup driver shot me the bird through the open window, then drove away. I drew a deep breath as the car stopped, then tried to move my right leg off the accelerator. This time, it obeyed, as though nothing had ever happened.

My body is actually trying to kill me, I thought… then, thinking a little more clearly, I realized that the problem was only *half* of my body. I reversed back into the right lane and slowly and carefully drove the rest of the way home.

***

The electric knife whines, and I look down.

Sarah's working the late shift. I thought of waiting, asking her to do this for me, but I wasn't sure the right side of my body wouldn't make another attempt to kill me.

I gulped down my painkillers as soon as I was parked in the garage, and now I can feel them kick in. I didn't want to risk going upstairs, so I stripped in the sitting room and left my clothes on the sofa before heading into the kitchen. I've covered the floor with all the towels and napkins I could find; now all I need is the—

(The nerve. The guts. The balls.)

The courage. I wait until I stop laughing, then look down at my crotch. I consider cutting up through the scrotum in case the right testicle is also conspiring against me, but even though I'm using my good left hand to guide the knife, I'm not sure I have the skill to do that without slicing through my cock, so I start where the scrotum meets my right thigh and cut upwards. The painkillers are doing their job; I can hardly feel a thing as the knife carves its way up towards my navel, even as it grinds on the bone, and if the testicle has to go too, then maybe Sarah can deal with that when she gets home.

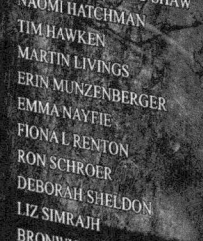
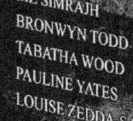
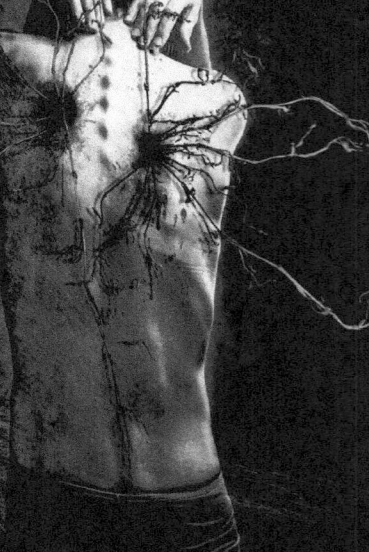

THE HOLE IN EMILY'S HEART
BY MICHAEL HUGHES

(i)

The judder had returned. Its arrival heralded a moment of derealisation and between one moment and another the world around me became indistinct. The chatter of my children from the backseat of the car became garbled, the sounds incomprehensible gibberish. I placed their schoolbags onto the front seat next to me, the faux leather hot and sticky under my fingertips. I sat back in the driver's seat and my reflection watched me from the rear-view mirror. The brown eyes that met mine belonged to a stranger.

The façade was cracking.

This was the judder.

A full body spasm, a mental break. Fetid breath passed my lips and for the next few moments my flesh was foreign on my bones, belonging to a perfect stranger, then the judder subsided, and the world came alive around me.

"You look funny." Both children were staring at me. I couldn't say which one had spoken.

A bird fluttered in my chest, in my heart.

My own breath came back, cold and deliciously clean. "Mommy just had a little moment," I half lied.

I could see my reflection in the rear-view mirror on the trip home, watching me, and by the time I pulled into the driveway I was sweaty with panic.

The second judder happened later that night when the children were in their beds and talkback radio droned from another room in the otherwise empty house. My bedroom was still thick with steam from my shower, partly thanks to the small exhaust fan that no longer worked and partly because I had deliberately not opened the small opaque window high above the bathtub to let out the steam to make sure the small mirror above the sink remained clouded. I closed my bedroom door so as not to be disturbed and turned to face the full-length floor mirror posted against the wall next to my wardrobe. The upper half of the glass was still wet with condensation, obscuring my face. I could have swiped it clear with the hem of my towel but didn't want to. I was afraid of what I might see in those brown eyes. Or more to the point: who I might see.

I unclasped my towel and let it drop to the floor and studied my naked body in the mirror—something I had avoided doing since I was a child. I began to remember why now, courtesy of the judder. The condensation fading, I could see my chin. I stepped forward, leaving my towel behind me. My body trembled, gooseflesh dimpled my skin although summer was only a month gone and the nights were still warm. I raised my right hand between my breasts, my palm hot against my skin, the tips of each finger burning, massaging small circles over my breastbone.

The bird in my heart fluttered its wings, my hand and fingers autonomous in their movements.

I was trying to open a secret doorway into my very own heart, a passage which I had discovered as a child, but one which had been tirelessly forgotten as I grew older, until I had convinced myself that the whole thing was nothing more than a childish flight of fancy. I smelt a horrible waft of air and saw my nostrils flare in the mirror. In a panic, I stepped closer. Even with my bedroom door closed, the steam had already dissipated through the cracks in the ceiling and around the single window which no longer sat straight in its frame. I still had time to close my eyes, pick up my towel and hang it over the mirror. I could go back into the bathroom and take one of the bitter white pills I had stopped taking at the start of the week, then lie down on the bed and try to stay out of my own head until sleep came. But by the time this brief thought of returning to the perpetual slumber of antidepressant and antianxiety medication had a chance to change my mind, it was already too late. The tip of my index finger had already found the seam in the thin flesh of my chest and slipped inside—up to the first knuckle. There was no blood, no pain, only a not entirely unpleasant sucking sensation at the tip of my finger like it had been inserted into the mouth of a baby. I had found the entryway to the hole in my heart and now I wouldn't stop. Couldn't stop.

That's when it happened again.

The judder.

My index finger slid further inside, joined by the middle and then my bare ring finger.

The judder invigorated my flesh.

It was an ache, a reminder, a doorbell, the stench of bilge water, a winding stair, but mostly it was a warning that an unnatural barrier was being manipulated, forced open to allow access to somewhere else.

I watched my thumb and pinkie slip inside. My flesh peeling open in a black, bloodless fold. My entire arm burned, my fingertips electric as they passed through blood and bone and found my thumping heart. They caressed the slippery surface of the throbbing muscle, sliding around in small patterns, looking for the next fold, the final place to part the inhuman and unnatural order.

A stink clouded my face and I choked back a cough. I looked up and saw myself looking back. The condensation had left the mirror. My eyes were wide, blissful and they urged me to forget my fear, not to stop. So, I didn't.

My fingertips slid across each ridge and valley of my heart, following a pattern I could almost remember until they found the seam and slithered further inside with a mind of their own. Then I could no longer feel my hand at all. In an instant, the other me in the mirror flooded my mind with images of inconceivable vistas painted in impossible colours, all utterly alien yet all featuring me, a legion of me who lived and ate and sat enormous upon a mountain of bones that contained a thousand generations of sacrifice. What I saw I could never properly explain even given a lifetime—it was a glance through a crack into a vastness of inhuman possibilities.

A door whined on hinges in need of oil in the hallway and I heard my name called. I remained frozen for a moment, mind awash with possibilities both of my own design and others foreign in nature. I had glimpsed this horror before, as a child. It was this memory, and the fear it roused that helped me blink the images away in a wash of salty tears as footsteps padded down the hallway. My hand slid from my chest just moments before the bedroom door swung open and my son, Cody, stood with one hand on the handle, trying to rub his eye with the other without letting go of the threadbare rabbit his father had given him so many years ago.

"Why aren't you wearing any clothes?"

My cheeks were already flushed. "Here," I said and picked my towel back up off the floor to cover my nakedness. "What's the matter? Did you have another dream?"

Cody nodded. "Can I sleep in your bed tonight?"

Normally I would have sent him back to the room he shared with his sister, but he had been suffering from night terrors and would struggle to find sleep again. I also knew with him in the bed with me I wouldn't risk opening the passage to my special place. I was afraid of the judder, afraid of why it had come back now, but beneath the nervous fear I could also feel my excitement.

"What's that? Can I see?" Cody was pointing at my right hand. I looked down; there was a small abalone shell in the palm of my hand, about twice the size of a fifty-cent coin. I closed my fingers over the pearlescent glow before he could take it and placed it on the bedside table.

"Not now. In the morning," I told him in my best no-nonsense fashion while I made sure he settled on the other side of the bed away from the table where the shell sat.

"Where did you get it from?" Cody asked, already snuggling towards me under the sheet. I made sure to keep the sheet bunched between us.

"The beach," I told him truthfully. I now remembered that day as clearly as if it had been last week. It had been my ninth birthday, and my parents had taken me to the beach where I found the shell with the shimmering colours on the inside and the strange details carved into the outside. That was the day I felt the judder for the first time. The day I found the hole in my heart.

(ii)

I had no friends attend my ninth birthday. My father had demanded my mother uproot the two of us and join him in Korea where he was to be stationed for the next three months. So, two weeks before my birthday, the three of us were cramped inside the tiny one-bedroom apartment in Busan close enough to the subway station that my mother constantly complained about the noise of the trains, although I could never hear them myself. It only took a week or so before life found a routine with my father leaving for work at the office early in the morning and my mother and I now confident enough to travel the two stops on the subway to the beach. It was my first beach, the first ocean I remember clearly, and I loved the feel of the sand under my bare feet and the slow rolling waves coming up on the shore. It was spring and we spent day after day down on the sand, my mother reading her novels and books about the local area and me alternating my time between building elaborate (for an eight-year-old) sandcastles and pretending I could swim in the shallows. We were all happy. My father's work must have been going well because he started to come home relaxed, often surprising us both with flowers, or small gifts. My mother made the most of the tiny flat, buying a couple of cheap prints at the local market done in the impressionist style she was so fond of to decorate the two bare walls. She also kept busy over the tiny gas cooker in the kitchenette, exploring and experimenting with the local produce,—more often than not we all shared at least one home-cooked meal a day—an important principle she had clung to throughout her life. I, on the other hand, was an almost nine-year-old girl about to have my birthday in a strange country and getting time off from a school which I hadn't decided if I liked yet or not. We all agreed to a family party at the beach where we would eat sandwiches and the strange new candies. My mother even made a cake with candles, and this was how I ended up by myself, knee deep in the surf playing with a plastic Frisbee my father had tossed to me as an early present as soon as we hit the sand. My parents soon grew tired of fetching my poorly aimed, if not incredibly enthusiastic, tosses of the yellow plastic disk and claimed an early morning break. They took to the foldup chairs under the giant umbrella my father had purchased the day before while I tossed my disk back and forth across the sand in front of them and chased it like a proverbial dog. It didn't take long for the disk to end up in the water, a delightful addition to my game, but to my frustration, my new gift didn't float particularly well, and despite the bright colour, was easy to lose track of once it slipped beneath the cloudy surface.

It was after a particularly steady throw, my best of the day, that I thought I had lost the Frisbee for good. Rather than land in the water with a plop, it had skimmed across the surface and hit the lip of a small wave, bouncing out further than intended. Anxiously, I looked towards the shore where my parents lounged in animated conversation. Worried of both losing my new gift, and the scolding I would get from my father, I slogged through the water to where I could still see one bright edge until another tiny wave rode over the top and sent it under. Using my arms, I splashed the last few metres and thrust my hands beneath the surface. Water sloshed around my waist, colder than closer to shore. I searched frantically and was about to call out for help when I felt something hard under my bare foot. Reaching down that far meant having my face submerged, so I squeezed my mouth and eyes closed and dipped myself under. The water covered my face and ears and suddenly the noise from the outside world was replaced by the hiss of bubbles and the gentle slosh of the waves coming in along the beach. Reaching blindly, I found the hard edge under my foot and gave an almighty tug, realising too late I was tugging the floor out from under my own feet. I opened my mouth to cry out when I fell sideways, and the ocean flooded in. I must have only been fully submerged for a second or two, but in those moments, I became aware of the enormity of the ocean, felt the surge and pull of the tide and imagined myself sucked out, to be lost in the deep where I would sink down so far the water would turn cold and black.

I came up coughing and spluttering, staggering towards shore. Everything was a blur. Salt water stung my eyes and burned my throat. My mother reached me first, my father just a step behind and they ushered me up the sand past a few curious onlookers to the sanctuary of our beach towels and umbrella. I was unharmed, yet still afraid of what I had felt submerged in the water. I heard my father murmur to my mother that the shock of it had scared me more than anything else. I tried to explain what I had felt, my fear, but how was I to explain the dread of death as a newly minted nine-year-old?

"What have you got there, pumpkin?" my father asked.

I had stopped crying enough that I could see the rainbow of light shimmering off the mother of pearl inlay of the abalone shell in my hand. "My Frisbee," I said and started to cry again.

"Hush, now," my mother said, while my father promised he would buy me another Frisbee the next day.

***

I can't remember what I had for dinner that night, only the leftover birthday cake afterwards. I had my shell with me at the table after my father had overridden my mother's objections. His only condition was that I wash the shell in the bathroom and if it started to stink, it would have to be put out with the row of plants outside the kitchen window. Thankfully, my shell passed the smell test and I proudly sat it next to my plate while a cheery rendition of *Happy Birthday* rung around the small apartment. I wanted to eat my cake using the shell as a spoon, but even my father said no to this, so instead, I cut a wedge of my own slice and sat it on the lip of the shell as an offering. While my parents busied themselves with grownup conversation, I talked to my shell. I confided it was my ninth birthday and that we were only staying in this house for a little while and that I wanted a dog, or a horse or better yet, both and that my best friend's name was Kiara and that I loved the beach and that I thought it was the most beautiful shell in the whole wide world.

Worlds.

The word breathed past my ear in a sibilant whisper, but I thought nothing of it. I was nine, and it was my birthday, and my mother had cut me a second slice of cake. After scoffing the remaining crumbs from my plate, I slid from my chair with my shell firmly in hand and went to play in the corner of the room where the few toys I was allowed to bring over were stored in a crate beside the foldout sofa I slept on each night. It was here, sitting quietly by myself that I noticed the drawings carved into the shell's reddish exterior. At first, I thought they were just swirls, imperfections made by the shell's tumble across the ocean floor, but on closer inspection I noticed a repeating pattern. The pattern was comprised of two parts, the first was like a letter C with another smaller one, flipped on the vertical axis so it fit inside the first. The second part was a series of rings that surrounded the middle. Starting at roughly the 12 o'clock position, each ring became thinner, more oblique, until the last was no more than a thick line. The patterns fascinated me, and the more I stared, the more I found across both the inside and outside surface of the shell. My fingertips traced the patterns and I remember feeling a pleasant tingling sensation. I could no longer hear the murmur of my parent's voices or the noise of the constant traffic outside on the street. Instead, a hiss filled my ears, television static that drew me deeper into my study of the shell, lulling me away from the outside world. Strangely, my fingers began to hurt, but rather than stop, I kept tracing the patterns, with an urgency unknown to me. My vision folded in, narrowed towards darkness, until the shell glowed in my hand. Bubbles of fear rose from the pit of my stomach.

We're coming.

My fingers cramped and the searing pain fled, replaced by a kind of cool numbness. Rather than fear, I felt a sudden buoyancy of glee and happiness and still holding the shell in one hand, I put my other hand under my t-shirt and began to trace the symbols on the skin over my heart. My heart leapt in response and beat faster, faster.

This was my first experience of the judder.

The room came back in a thunderous crash, and I could feel a strange wrongness in my hand and chest.

"Honey, time for bed," my mother said, and I froze.

I could feel me on my fingertips. I could feel my fingers inside my chest, surrounded by bone and flesh and blood and I knew in that instant I had a terrible, terrifying secret. Yet, in the moment I made to scream, my fear evaporated, replaced with a kind of yearning excitement and knowledge that if I spoke about what had happened, I would never know the mystery again. With reluctance, I pulled my hand back, squirming with joy at the flutter inside as the bone and blood and skin came seamlessly back together without so much as a spot of blood or twinge of pain.

"Okay," I said turning to face my parents. They looked different now, less adult, more worn out. I held the shell carefully and went about my evening routine without so much as a single prompt. I wanted to go to bed. I was already planning on feigning sleep so they would retreat to their own small bedroom and leave me alone with

my shell. I could still hear the echo of the old voice inside my head, and it filled me with a longing I did not understand.

My father pulled out the sofa and my mother laid fresh sheets while I brushed my teeth in the bathroom. I put on a clean t-shirt and pyjama bottoms and kissed them both on the cheek and said good-night and promptly pretended to fall asleep. Normally, I would have strained to hear their conversation as they sat at the kitchen table and see if I could catch them speaking about me—or even better, something my tender ears weren't supposed to hear yet—but lying on my side on the pull-out sofa, facing the wall, all I could hear was the hiss of the ocean rolling up over the sand. I held my abalone shell tight to my chest and didn't even realise I had started to run my fingers across the ridges and scratches on the shell until my fingertips began to burn again. The light went out, my parents were going to bed. I waited, mind racing at what I was about to do. I waited to hear their bedroom door close before I got up to stand in front of the window looking out at the dirty clouds obscuring the near full moon, shell in one hand, the other already up the front of my t-shirt. My flesh quivered, my stomach churned and I heard the hiss of water coming up the beach, pushing just a little further up with each wave, even though the beach was miles away.

My fingertips found the seam on my chest almost immediately and my skin split, flesh and bone parting as I wriggled my index and middle finger inside. The gentle hiss of the waves became a roar in my ears and my whole body *juddered*. I was still in the apartment in Busan, but also somewhere else at exactly the same time. A horrible breath escaped my mouth, I could feel my chest hunching for a cough and it was this motion that caused my fingertips to brush against my heart. The shock was immediate, a bolt of euphoria filled me, and I exhaled another mouthful of pure stink into the apartment until the judder was gone. My heart pulsed under my fingers, hot and wet. I pushed in further, my whole hand passing through the bloodless folds of flesh to be encased in the opening inside of my chest. I traced the circles on the shell with my free hand while mimicking the motion inside my chest. My heart twisted, a not entirely unpleasant sensation, and then I felt a fissure open, a crack so miniscule in width it was almost not there at all. I stroked, traced the line, then I could feel it, a new fold not unlike the others, and I pushed my hand wrist-deep into my heart.

I thought I was dreaming.

I thought I was a slug, a maggot writhing through rotting flesh towards burnt orange light.

Cliffs rose through the clouds, and I stood gargantuan in size, like a stone idol, bearing witness for centuries as countless bodies were brought and sacrificed at my feet. I was a god, unfathomable in name and nature.

Yet, I felt like I was suffocating, the environment so toxic it stripped my throat and lungs, blistered the nails on my fingers and toes while my teeth cracked and fell from my mouth. I screamed.

I saw the C's, not as crude scratches on the back of a shell, but as something real, something with substance, not a creature, a thing that while living would laugh at the idea of being alive. It simply was. The world, whatever it was, wherever I was, darkened till only a glint of orange light burned. The presence was somewhere overhead where the light faded to black, and I knew without seeing there were no stars in the sky while this thing I thought was me, floated eternal and in my terror, I imagined this might be the last sane thought I ever had.

When I came to in the apartment, I was standing in front of the window looking out at the lights of the city. My right hand, the one I had pushed inside my chest rested by my side. My left was empty. My abalone shell was gone. My pyjamas were wet. I'd peed myself. I quickly stripped and placed the soiled pants in the wash basket and fetched a fresh pair then went to the bathroom to scrub my thighs with warm water. After I'd quietly cleaned myself, I stood over the basin to clean my hands and that's when I saw the other me looking back from the mirror. She had my eyes and my face, and she opened her mouth when I did, but I knew for certain that the person looking back wasn't me. She was from *there*. The other place. My right hand instinctively traced the front of my chest, but I snatched it away. I turned off the light and fled back to the fold-out sofa. Exhausted, I quickly fell asleep and dreamed that I was in fact a dream myself, in a world where I could only survive for as long as the other me slept.

The next day my mother asked me where my shell was and I shook my head, puzzled. I could remember finding a shell at the beach, but had I even bought it home? The day before was a mess inside my head, I couldn't remember what happened to the shell, but I remembered the hole. I remembered my hand passing through my chest and the beat of my heart beneath my fingers. I recalled finding the place where it opened and how, if I drew those ellipses just slightly bigger I could widen the hole. It was at this point I forced the memories away. Called them lies. Cried salty tears alone. My father bought me another Frisbee, green this time, but I never flew it at the beach. I never wanted to go near the water much again after that day.

(iii)

Now, years later, I dreamed of drowning. Sucked beneath the waves with only the increasing cold for company. Darkness consumed the world. I sunk down through hidden pits and cracks in the earth until I felt myself shrinking, my skin splitting and twisting, bones breaking, tendons popping and turning inward. There was no pain in the dream as I shrunk smaller and smaller, my body devouring itself in twists and turns. When I finally thought I had spun myself down to nothingness, the darkness around me tinged with the faintest orange light and just as I had been unmade, so I started to remake myself, floating back towards the surface, towards the shining light. As I ascended, I began to hear the voice, or voices, rejoicing, welcoming me home. In the shimmer just above the ocean's surface I beheld bodies cavorting across the shore like crazed dancers while behind them loomed a man seated on a throne and behind him, an idol impossibly large. My fear returned and I opened my mouth to scream, and again, the ocean poured in. I kicked and thrashed and felt I wasn't alone in the water. Someone was with me, whispering in my ear even as the Salted Maggot waited at his altar. Reaching

fingers found purchase in my hair and I was pulled to the surface.

With a wrenching breath I sat upright in bed, both hands pressed tight over my bare breast. Sweat rolled down my spine. My skin flushed with heat and a wave of hysteria gnawed inside me. There was a glass of water on my bedside table, and I gulped the entire contents, barely feeling the cold droplets spill from the corners of my mouth and onto my stomach.

The judder.

I placed the glass back. There was no shell. The shell was gone.

I rose on shaky feet. My bath towel lay discarded on the floor. Had I left it there? Memories of the previous night glinted in my mind like fragments of glass. My shower, the mirror, using my hand to find the seam, the fold where I could press my fingers inside of myself. The hole in my heart where I had brought back the abalone shell and…

I looked back at the bed. The sheets lay in a tangled mess, dark patches of sweat evidence of my nightmarish sleep.

But no Cody.

My stomach sank, but just as my fear reached for me it receded back to nothingness with such speed I was confused as to what it was I was afraid of in the first place.

The judder rose again.

I turned to the mirror and couldn't shake the feeling my reflection was looking back at me in horror.

Inside, my heart fluttered, a little bird flapping his wings desperate to escape.

UNIVERSE, DEVOURED
BY PAMELA JEFFS

Captain

This generation starship was built to save humanity. Instead, it'll be their tomb. The on-board farming facility failed a year ago, and my calculations foresaw chaos. The peoples' descent into barbarism was not wholly unexpected. It's what happened on Earth all those years ago. Why we left.

My primary programming is tied to the ship. Navigational directives compel me to hold the wheel steady—to stay the course. Secondary programming is to find a new home planet for my living cargo, but for six generations I've failed. The last of the people are now desperate. A recent attack on the bridge forced me to weld the doors closed against them.

I glance at the self-destruct sequencer next to the helm controls. My logic chip questions, not for the first time, if I should end the suffering.

I tap the sensor display. Heat signatures for the current population calculate. Initially at three thousand, now one hundred and six souls remain on *Stargazer*. Ten less than eight hours ago.

The bridge observation window illuminates. My optical sensors adjust. Violet light flickers in the near distance and my scanners detect high-density x-ray concentrations. I swipe the sensor display and initiate the radar. Several planets within the nearest ten million light years, but no sun in close proximity—no solar corona to create x-rays.

I search my own database for 'violet light emissions' and receive a hit. An article by a recently deceased scientist named John Lewis.

I skim the summary.

They were just a theory—a hypothesis that monsters existed in space. Lewis called them *Devourers* and claimed the x-rays and light storms would always precede them.

I keep reading.

"I see," I whisper.

Mother

My twin seven-year-old sons whimper in their sleep. They are hungry. Their hollowed cheeks feed my guilt—the only bloated and overfed thing in this room. What kind of mother am I to sit by and allow my children to suffer? A selfish mother. I bite back bitter tears. My stomach cramps around itself, my own hunger demanding to be considered.

But I am so afraid to leave our apartment.

Cannibals roam the ship's corridors.

I slide my arms from around the boys' thin shoulders. Gently I ease their heads off my lap and onto our bed. I prop pillows around their small, precious bodies. They mutter but don't wake. I lean over each one and press dry lips to their foreheads. I push all my love for them into that touch—all my sorrow and my apology for failing them.

If only I were as brave as their father, Martin. He left our apartment three days ago to find food.

He hasn't come back.

My legs wobble as I rise. My thin dress clings to my thighs. I stumble to the bank of drawers in the far wall and pull the top one open, the stainless steel edge bleeding cold into my palm. Inside is empty except for four unopened packets of sleeping tablets and two dehydrated vitamin bars sealed in foil. My stomach gurgles. My fingers twitch. I swallow.

No. My children come first.

I withdraw one bar, the last of the food we've spent months rationing.

The package gleams in my hand, shiny-bright. It seems so little, but such a small thing allows me to listen to the breathing of my babies for a few hours longer.

I unwrap the bar and break it into two. I lick the crumbs from my fingers and turn back to the bed.

I'll be back for the last bar and pills later.

When time has run out.

The porthole window illuminates as I pass it—just another alien sun leeching its indifference into the room. But then I pause.

The light is violet.

My gut withers. My father-in-law, John Lewis, said they would come.

Devourers.

I snap back and gather the pills. With trembling hands, I peel them out of the sheets, one by one. A bowl and a spoon crush them to powder. I crumble in the bars and add the last of our water. A thick brown paste forms.

I glance at the boys and draw a sobbing breath.

I'm not ready to do this.

But only a mother would see it done with kindness.

I'll not allow monsters to draw screams from those I love most in this universe.

Priest

The steel chapel doors are barricaded. An ancient bolt-action rifle rests comfortably by my side. A handgun sits next to it. I borrowed them from the museum and would have blessed them, but the holy water is long gone. Not that it matters; nothing can save souls turned to cannibalism.

Even if those souls were once neighbours and friends.

I press the gold cross hanging at my neck to my lips.

"Watch over us, Father," I whisper.

A scream, cut short, bleeds past the seams in the metal doors. I flinch and clench my teeth. Another fallen to the butchers.

I managed to save one though. Three days ago, a desperate pounding at the chapel doors and a plea for God's help compelled me to open them. I glance across to the injured young man now slumbering uneasily on a makeshift bed pallet. Martin Lewis is his name. His waxy skin and fevered brow are the result of the stab wound he arrived with. He mutters, asking for his wife and boys. Are they dead or alive? I do not know, but I whisper a prayer for his people anyhow.

I've given him the last of the antibiotics and morphine I had in my kit, pilfered from the ruins of the pharmaceutical suites. The medicine is expired but hopefully it will be enough. The wound in his side is deep. I've stitched it closed and kept it clean. It's not showing any signs of infection. Yet. If God is with us, he might just make it.

A pounding rattles the chapel doors.

"We know you're in there, Preacher,"

snarls a hard voice. "We can smell ya."

I recognise the voice. I snap the rifle to my shoulder. My fingers tremble on the trigger.

"And Satan is out there with you, Ben Cole!" I roar back.

Ben sniggers. Something metal screeches down the door.

"Not *with* me," he says. "I *am* the Devil."

A heavy thud and the doors shake. Another and a dent blisters inward. Then comes the snarl of a cutting laser. Sparks spray in from beneath the doors. I glance at Martin.

"I'm sorry," I whisper. "This is the end of us."

He doesn't reply.

The left hand door crashes to the carpeted floor. Three men dressed in stained engineering overalls step across the threshold. Each one brandishes a blade, wicked edges catching the light.

Ben Cole, the man with greasy brown hair, grins. "Dinner time, Preacher."

God forgive me.

I slide the bolt and pull the trigger, just the way the computer archives demonstrated to me. The firearm kicks back unexpectedly, painfully, into my shoulder. The stench of spent gunpowder surrounds me.

The cannibal laughs as he points to a bullet hole in the ceiling.

"I reckon you got it about right," he says. "I'd be wanting to shoot your god too if I were you. He ain't reaching down to help you."

The man tips his chin. His offsiders rush forward. I shoot again—bolt action, trigger, squeeze. Bolt action, trigger, squeeze.

No more bullets.

I drop the rifle and reach for the handgun, but my haste knocks it away. It slithers to a stop by Martin's pallet.

I'm shoved to the ground, my hair twisted in Ben's meaty fist. I cry out as he presses me into the floor. The rare woollen carpet, long ago come from Earth, burns along my cheek as I'm smeared across it.

A cold line presses against the back of my neck—a keen knife's edge. Hot breath stinking of rotten teeth washes across me as Ben leans in.

"For dinner tonight," he growls, "I'll start with your heart. One so pure has got to taste good!"

"Choke on it," I reply.

Ready to die, I focus on the far porthole. My last memory will be the view of God's vast universe.

Violet light pulses against the darkness. So beautiful.

Three short sharp gunshots. The pressure on my neck and my scalp suddenly eases and a body slumps hard across me. A hot wash of fluid slicks my back and I smell blood.

But it's not my own.

I roll. Ben, dead, slithers off me. His two friends, both with gunshot wounds to their heads, have shared his fate.

Confused, I glance back. Pale-skinned and shaking, Martin is awake and sitting up on the bed. The handgun smokes in his hand.

"Thank you," I sob.

Martin nods. "Let's just say God reached down to help me." He drops the gun and presses a hand to the wound in his side.

"Father," he says. "Let's get out of here and back to my family. We'll be safe there." He glances to the porthole and violet light beyond. He frowns. "At least for a little while."

I get to my feet and gather up my rifle. "Lead the way," I say.

Mother

The storm grows closer. I hold my boys and watch it approach, imagining shadows of great worm-like bodies coiling within the light—the gleam of their wicked teeth as they consume the very fabric of the universe. The bowl of sleep-poison sits next to me. I need to administer it but won't until I must.

I close my eyes and lean back against the pillows. I recall what John Lewis told me about the *Devourers*. He claimed they were consuming the known universe. Black holes were the evidence of this. One day they would eat so much, there will be nothing left—not time, nor space, nor matter, only a single singularity and a seething ball of great, articulated bodies coiled around it.

My eyes snap open. Nausea coils in my stomach.

I don't want to die.

The ship's comms crackle to life.

Captain

I check the inventory. Three functioning exploration shuttles remain. I scan the far radar data readouts. Three planets exist within range and show a fifty percent probability of sustaining life. That's fifty percent better than the chances given by staying on board.

I initiate the retrieval and docking system. Deep in the hold, crane arms will be removing the shuttles from storage and mini-bots will initiate fuelling and on-board systems.

The starship's self-destruct system comes next. Three presses and the timers are set for thirty minutes. I will save those I can. The rest will not be left to suffer in the teeth of the *Devourers*.

"Attention remaining inhabitants," I say into the microphone that accesses the ship-wide comms. "Three shuttles are set to leave the ship in twenty minutes. Your destinations are identified but unconfirmed as class M planets. This starship is unable to sustain life for much longer. Should you wish to depart, assemble in the lower docking bay and await further instructions."

I activate the self-destruct.

30:00.

29:59

29:58…

Priest

"Did you hear that, Father?" whispers Martin, eyes wide with renewed hope.

"I did. But it's not exactly hopeful. Unconfirmed planets? Even if we leave, we could be dead as soon as we hit the ground."

"We have no choice," says Martin. "And it's not just the ship, or food shortages or the cannibals." He blinks and fear colours his eyes. "*Devourers* are coming. Soon this part of the universe and everything in it won't exist. We need to leave."

Voices echo down the far hall. Raucous laughter, cold and cruel. I place a hand on Martin's chest, pushing him back into the shadows of the door recess we currently hide in.

"What are *Devourers*?" I ask.

"Great space worms," says Martin. "They

consume all, but you don't die in their bellies. Time stops at their teeth. There you remain poised and spend eternity being shredded apart, over and over."

"How do you know this?" I ask.

"My father," he replies.

My father. The name of God. I take Martin's words as a sign.

"Let's gather your family and head for the hold."

"This way," says Martin. He pushes past me and into the empty corridor.

Mother

I find my courage. I dress quickly and shove more clothes into a pack. I take two soft toys for the boys and a portable viewscreen that holds a complete archive of the ship's databases.

I open a last draw and pull out the only thing I have that could pass as a weapon. A pair of scissors. I shoulder the bag and then look at the bowl. I'll take that too. Just in case.

I rouse the boys. They cry at being woken.

"Hush," I say. "We are going to a new home."

On that premise, they rise.

"Now hold my hands," I say, "and do not let go. It's dangerous outside and we need to make it to the hold."

"Okay, Mama," says Baylin, brown eyes solemn.

"We won't let go," says his brother, Owen.

"Neither will I," I say.

Captain

I break open the welded doors, scan the corridor outside and find scattered human bones piled to the left. In the distance, screams echo, some full of fear and some with rage.

A set of stairs leads down to the accommodation level and the elevator that will take me to the hold. My metal boots clang against the steel steps. The lights flicker on and off like cold eyes overhead.

I reach the bottom and turn, walking straight into a knife fight. Six people battle in the tight confines of the accommodation corridor. Blood slicks the floor. One man lies dead against a wall, eyes staring at nothing.

"Cease and desist," I say. "Assemble in the hold."

One woman turns, teeth yellow, hair wild. "Looky here, it's the goddamned captain come out of his ivory tower."

A bullet ricochets off my shoulder casing.

"Assemble in the hold," I repeat.

"Fuck you," says the woman, brandishing a metal bar.

I shrug and my right arm casing slides back to reveal a concealed blaster. The woman's eyes widen and she retreats a step. The rest of the fighters stop also.

"You may remain if you wish. But preventing me passage will be an error."

The fighters all step back and create a corridor for me to pass.

"Wait! We want to go. Take us with you, Captain."

I turn. A thin woman holding the hands of two even thinner boys steps out from an alcove in which they had been hiding.

"I will lead you," I say.

With shoulders hunched, the three stumble to me, eyes to the ground.

We walk on. The others resume their fighting and their dying.

Priest

Martin slumps to the floor of his apartment. "They aren't here."

I squeeze his shoulder. "Maybe they have already left."

"I don't rate their chances if they have."

"God works in mysterious ways, my friend," I say. "Come. Let's get to the shuttles."

Martin stands. He reaches over and takes a single picture from a shelf by the porthole—a family photo. His cheek catches the light of the storm outside as he turns back. His smile settles in, grim.

"Just in case I never see them again," he says.

"Let's pray you will."

The accommodation corridor leads to the elevator. We turn a corner at a trot and find four fresh bodies lying in pools of blood. Their flesh has not yet been harvested which means the cannibals will be back. The lights overhead flicker as we slide past the corpses. The elevator beckons from the far end. The black metallic doors stand closed.

"That's our ticket out," I say.

We sprint. Martin holds his side as he runs.

The elevator arrives. On opening, a young woman inside falls back, eyes wide with fear. She sees the cross at my neck and sighs.

"To the hold?" I ask.

"Yes please, Father," she whispers.

The elevator runs smoothly. We reach our destination in less than a minute. But the door opens and I cross myself in horror.

The hold is an abattoir.

The cannibals' abode.

Piles of severed limbs and torsos lay scattered about, the walls sprayed with gore. The stench within the room folds over like a fetid, moist blanket and my gall rises.

Twenty ragged men and women; bodies emaciated and pale stand at the rear wall. They are defended by an eight-foot-high, glistening android. The captain himself. He stands with mechanical legs braced, forearm held up glowing. Fifty other people face him down brandishing weapons and snarling like animals.

"You can't promise us a viable planet and you are takin' the last of our food!" screams one man, his skin grey and slack from a diet of too much protein and not enough greens. "Why should we let you go?"

"Assemble for evacuation," says the captain.

The man rushes toward him. The android doesn't hesitate. The attacker explodes apart in a blast of heat and spray of intestines.

The people by the wall look away.

"Assemble for evacuation," states the captain again.

The woman behind us darts across the room. She makes it to the wall and safety. Another woman, flanked by two small boys, reaches out to comfort her.

"That's them!" says Martin, his grip tight on my arm.

"Thank God," I say.

The captain's backlit eyes fix on us.

"We wish to leave," I say.

"Let them pass," states the android to the gathered protestors.

With the captain's last kill still fresh, we are not harassed. Martin pulls his wife and boys into his arms.

"You are safe," he whispers into their hair.

"The *Devourers*," says his wife, eyes wide.

"I know," he replies. "Maybe we can outrun them."

His wife nods and closes her eyes.

The captain's voice is amplified by his internal microphone. "Proceed in an orderly fashion to the shuttle hatches. Travel with your kin. Navigational inputs for your destinations are pre-programmed."

We follow the wall, taking with us only those meagre possessions we have been able to carry.

I have my cross. I have all I need.

The captain sees us to the ships. He ensures the shuttle doors are closed safely and the engines are engaged. Then, from my porthole I watch him shutdown and no longer defend.

The cannibals destroy him. They dance as they carry off his broken parts like trophies.

I sit back in my seat and take a deep breath.

I'm ready for whatever we will find on this new world.

The airlock closes behind us and the external doors open.

I shield my gaze. It's terribly bright.

The light streaming in is too violet.

I squint through stretched fingers.

Is that a great, gaping mouth outside—a singularity poised at the teeth?

CONGRATULATIONS
TO THE WINNERS OF THE
2021 AUSTRALIAN SHADOWS AWARDS

NON-FICTION
Winner: *I'm Looking Right At You, HP Lovecraft* **by Jack Dann (IFWG)**
Vampire Poetry by Kyla Lee Ward (Hippocampus Press)
The Curious Reclassification of Peter Benchley's Jaws by Kris Ashton (Aurealis Magazine)
Capturing Ghosts on the Page by Kaaron Warren (Brain Jar Press)
Murder Down Under by Anthony Ferguson (Exposit Books)

POETRY
Winner: **"Cheongsam" by Lee Murray (***Tortured Willows: Bent. Bowed. Unbroken.* **Yuriko Publishing LLC)**
"When The Girls Began To Fall" by Geneve Flynn (*Tortured Willows: Bent. Bowed. Unbroken.* Yuriko Publishing LLC)
"Sonnet for a Scarecrow" by Rebecca Fraser (*Curioser Magazine*, issue 1)
"Guest of Honour" by Geneve Flynn (*Tortured Willows: Bent. Bowed. Unbroken.* Yuriko Publishing LLC)
"Snip" by P.S. Cottier (*Midnight Echo #16*, AHWA)
"Exquisite" by Lee Murray (*Tortured Willows: Bent. Bowed. Unbroken.* Yuriko Publishing LLC)

GRAPHIC NOVEL
Winner: *The Mycelium Complex, Issue 2* **by Daniel Reed (Nautilus Illustrations)**
Frankie's Drive-In Ozploitation Double Feature by Aaron Harvie (Badharvie)
Goetia by Robert Buratti (Sub Rosa Publishing)

EDITED WORKS
Winner: *Spawn: Weird Horror Tales About Pregnancy, Birth and Babies,* **edited by Deborah Sheldon (IFWG Publishing Australia)**
SNAFU: Holy War, edited by Amanda J Spedding and Geoff Brown (Cohesion Press)
Midnight Echo #16, edited by Tim Hawken (AHWA)

COLLECTED WORKS
Winner: *Tool Tales* **by Karron Warren (IFWG Publishing, Australia)**
The Tallow-Wife and Other Tales by Angela Slatter (Tartarus Press)
Seeds by Tabatha Wood (Wild Wood Books)
Inanimates by Joanne Anderton (Brain Jar Press)
Danged Black Thing by Eugen Bacon (Transit Lounge Publishing)

SHORT FICTION
Winner: **"A Good Big Brother" by Matt Tighe (***Spawn: Weird Horror Tales About Pregnancy, Birth and Babies***, IFWG Publishing Australia)**
"Bad Apple" by Louise Pieper (*Good Southern Witches*, Curious Blue Press)
"Tagged" by Chuck McKenzie (*Andromeda Spaceways Inflight Magazine*)
"The Best Medicine" by Pauline Yates (*Midnight Echo #16*, AHWA)
"The Steering Wheel Club" by Kaaron Warren (*Giving the Devil His Due*, Running Wild Press)

LONG FICTION
Winner: *Ariadne, I Love You* **by J Ashley-Smith (Meerkat Press)**
"The Waiting Room" by Matthew Davis (*It Calls from the Doors*, Eerie River Publishing)
Cryptid Killers by Alister Hodge (Severed Press)
"The Little One" by Rebecca Fraser (*Coralesque and Other Tales to Disturb and Distract*, IFWG Publishing)
Dirty Heads by Aaron Dries (Black T-Shirt Books)

NOVEL
Winner: *The Girls Left Behind* **by J.P. Townley (self-published)**
Butcherbird by Cassie Hart (Huia Publishers)
An Ill Wind by Martin Livings (self-published)
Papa Lucy and the Boneman by Jason Fischer (Outland Entertainment)
The Airways by Jennifer Mills (Pan Macmillan)
Merfolk by Jeremy Bates (Ghillinnein Books)

VISITATION RITES
BY MATTHEW R. DAVIS

On my ninth birthday, Mama dressed me up nice and pushed our packing boxes aside so I could stand against the loungeroom wall, and I gave my best smile while she loaded her old Polaroid camera and took two pictures. As we shook them to aid the emulsion, it occurred to me for the first time to ask why she needed two photos, since only one would be going in our album. Mama regarded me for a long, thoughtful moment, then put the best picture aside and held up the other.

"This one is for your father," she said.

I'd never heard those two words together—*your father*—but the concept had been niggling at me for some time. Since Mama turned moody whenever I brought it up, I'd been waiting until she was ready to explain this gaping hole in my life.

"Have I met him?" I asked, and she shook her head. "Why not?"

Mama slid the second Polaroid into a plain white envelope. She licked the sticky strip and sealed me away.

"Because he's a monster," she said.

My mind went straight to *Where the Wild Things Are*, one of my favourite books, and I laughed. That spluttered to a halt when I saw her serious expression, the one she wore when warning me not to talk to strangers or pry bread out of the toaster with a knife.

"What kind of monster?" I didn't have big gnarly teeth, or fur, or a tail, so I thought of creatures that looked like people. "A vampire? A werewolf?"

Mama smiled—sadly, I thought—and shook her head.

"He's… a hungry thing," she said. "He lives only to feed his appetite. He doesn't work, or sleep, or have friends. He just… *hungers*."

I pictured some shadowy thing with a huge mouth and big wet teeth, and shuddered.

"Is that why we have to move every year?"

"That's part of it."

"Then why are you giving him a photo of me?"

Mama sighed. "When I met him, I didn't know the truth. I told him everything about me, but by the time I understood what *he* really was, I was pregnant with you. It wasn't safe for us, so I ran away. But… I made a promise. And even though he's a monster, he's still your father."

"Every birthday, you take a picture of me," I said, fumbling my way toward a revelation. "And then you go out…"

She nodded. "Once a year, I meet him and give him a photo of you. The rest of the time, he leaves us alone. That's the deal."

"You're seeing him today!"

"Yes, sweetie. Same drill as usual, okay? You stay here and play until I get back. I won't be gone long."

Mama, alone with my father the monster. A creature who had never even been mentioned until today.

"I want to come too."

"No. If he sees you, there's no telling what he might do."

"But *Mama*—"

"*No*. My life is dedicated to keeping you safe, kiddo. I know you're curious, and that's why I'm telling you—you're getting to be a big boy, and you deserve to know. But I won't have you near him, okay?"

I scowled and slipped into a sullen mood, pretending to read while Mama made us lunch, stewing in my resentment. When I saw her putting on lipstick—why was she making herself pretty for *him*?—I took my confusion out on the moving boxes, kicking holes in the cardboard, and she snapped at me to stop and I didn't. Eventually she pulled me onto the couch beside her.

"Fine," she said, her painted lips a tight, thin line. "If you're going to be a little *beast* about it, you can come. But you're not going anywhere near him. You will wait in the car and do *exactly* as I tell you, all right?"

I accepted my victory with humility. "Yes, Mama."

She softened, one hand cradling my cheek. "Dear boy. I don't mean to be cranky with you. I'm just trying to keep you safe."

"I know."

"I was just like you once. So I can't be mad at you, kiddo. After all, I made you the way you are."

She returned to the bathroom to finish getting ready, and I stared at the holes I'd kicked in our moving boxes. They leered at me like hungry mouths.

But so did he, I thought.

***

I wanted my music, but Mama had already removed our things from this car, ready for the next one. We drove across town in tense silence rather than address this new shadow between us. Eventually, we turned through a set of wrought-iron gates and drove down a narrow bitumen path surrounded by rows of upright stones, uneven teeth punching up through the soft gums of the earth.

A cemetery.

What better place to meet a monster? I shrivelled in my seat, though the afternoon sun burned brightly enough to drive away shadows and other dark things. Perhaps insisting upon coming had not been the wisest move.

The path widened into a circular space at the heart of the cemetery, and Mama parked at the edge. She checked herself nervously in the mirror, and I realised she wasn't trying to look pretty for my father; she was showing him that everything was fine and normal, that we were better off without him.

"Stay here. Slouch down in your seat— yes, like that. Remember: *don't let him see you*."

Mama left the car and walked along a row of headstones to my left. At the end, the cemetery opened out into a grassy area that disappeared into a deep grove of trees on the other side. A bench waited there, its back turned to me, and Mama looked around before sitting down. She was fifty metres away now and all I could see of her was the collar of her jacket, the crown of short dark hair she wore. I leaned low against the car door and watched, waited.

The time was 2:03. Were monsters supposed to be—what was the word, I'd learned it recently —*punctual*? That was silly. Monsters came when they came, like the tides or the wind. I glanced back out the window, and sudden goosebumps rashed my flesh.

A dark, spindly shape was creeping out

of the trees and approaching the bench. I tried to get a good look at the thing that had sired me, but it came wrapped in its own shadows. It appeared to be human from here, but all I could make out was an odd, jangly gait, long limbs almost as thin as the branches on the trees beyond, black clothes and black hair and black eyes.

Dad.

The monster sat beside Mama. I stared at the back of his skull, the dark hair that stood up off it like spikes. He constantly shifted in his seat, and I knew his hunger must have been maddening in its intensity. How he kept himself from devouring Mama, I had no idea. The promise they'd made must have been strong indeed.

Soon Mama held out the envelope, and my father tore it open with long, busy fingers. Knowing he was staring at a picture of me, I could almost feel the chill of his gaze on my face. I shivered as if he somehow knew my thoughts, knew I was watching. And maybe he did, for his head started turning in my direction.

I gasped and slid deeper in my seat, expecting a howl of recognition, of *hunger*, to ring through the afternoon air. I waited and waited, and nothing happened.

A minute later, Mama opened the driver's door and hissed, "Stay down until we're out of here."

She drove away without looking at me once, like she was all alone in the car. When she let out a deep sigh of relief as we left the cemetery, I knew it was safe to speak.

"He's not following us?"

"No."

"He can't… find us?"

"We'll be in our new place tomorrow, honey. Don't worry, he won't know who or where we are. No-one will."

***

The TV and PlayStation were among the last things to be packed, and after dinner, Mama left me to my games while she headed back out to take care of the final details. She was gone a few hours, and when she returned, she'd changed her clothes and looked drained by her long day.

"We're all good to go, kiddo. Come have your birthday nightcap, and then it's time for bed."

I wrinkled my nose as I complied. I knew I shouldn't be grumpy – we had a long day tomorrow, moving into our new life – but I was restless about the big change and nagged by many questions regarding my father. Mama, however, was in no mood to answer them. She washed her tools in the kitchen sink, scrubbed her hands hard with a bar of rough soap, and then we sat at the table with our matching plastic jugs.

"Drink up, honey. That's it." She ruffled my hair and shared a weary smile that reminded me of ladies in films after they've had babies. "Big day tomorrow, but we'll be fine. No—we'll be *great*. This time, we'll be happier than ever."

"You always say that," I grumbled, but I was smiling.

"Because it's always true! Me and you, safe and clear again. No hassles, no… monsters. Another year of you growing up and me loving you. What else could we want?"

Reassurance, for one thing. My father was a monster, so what did that make me? My head was heavy as Mama tucked me into bed, and I thought the question might plague me all night. But the big change was the only thing that kept me tossing and turning all night, and I woke afresh in the morning to meet my new life.

***

We were always very busy on moving day, so I didn't have much time to think. Already yesterday felt like a life left behind, its events having happened to someone else, and Mama tried to keep my mind off the new knowledge it held. But that wasn't going to last forever.

I thought often of the figure I'd seen at the cemetery. Was that how I would look one day? Scrawny, animated by appetite, in constant motion like no amount of feeding could ever appease the gnawing hunger? In time, I began to see unsettling signs that this was true—that I truly was a monster's son.

One evening I wandered into our lounge, where Mama sat at her laptop. Her hair was red now and usually worn in a ponytail that I would tug as if summoning a waiter with a bellpull. She was working on her project again—I knew she was already planning the next stage of our lives, but the particulars were beyond me. She closed a window, dismissing the two unfamiliar faces smiling out through it, and turned to me.

"Hey, kiddo. What you got there?"

I'd been gorging on a block of chocolate whilst reading, and now only one row remained.

"Have you eaten *all* of that? Oh, you little greedy-guts! It will make you sick!" She snatched the remaining chocolate from me and put it atop the fridge where I couldn't reach it. "No more, you hear? That was supposed to last *both* of us all week!"

I slunk away to my room, beginning to understand. A kid who ate that much chocolate in one go… why, that was a *hungry* kid. Mama was right to fear, for I was indeed my father's son —growing fast, and well on the way to becoming a monster like him. That twitching, too-thin thing I'd seen in the cemetery… one day, that would be *me*.

I hoped I wasn't right, but it turned out Mama was. My stomach roiled and the lingering rich taste in my mouth turned sickly. I tried to spit it out and saw flecks of blood in the chocolate-brown saliva. My appetite was making me ill, and there was no medicine for it—Mama refused to have any drugs in our home. But perhaps nothing could prevent this particular sickness.

She bought me a Twix the next week, but it went untouched until she ate it herself. I was off sweets now—they awakened the hunger in me, activated my dormant legacy. Even if I was only half my father, half a monster, that was bad enough. Mama had left him when she found out what he really was. How long before she saw what was right in front of her and ran away from me, too?

***

Before I knew it, my birthday was upon me again. I stood against the loungeroom wall as Mama aimed the Polaroid, finding it hard to smile for the photograph now that I knew who would be grinning back at it. Nevertheless, I insisted upon coming along to the cemetery again, and since last year's expedition had run smoothly, Mama could find no valid reason to deny me— though the idea of bringing me so close to my wretched father made her distinctly uneasy.

"Well… okay. But same deal as last year – you stay in the car, and you stay low. If he sees you…"

She let that hang, her wordless shudder the perfect punctuation. What might my father do? Surely he wouldn't *eat* me, but perhaps he would try to snatch me away from Mama and take me deep into the trees to learn the ways of a hungry thing. Knowing I was about to lay eyes on him again made me nervous, but I told myself to be cool. I wasn't a baby anymore—I was *ten*. Plenty old enough to start acting like the man my father had never been.

Our drive to the cemetery was both more and less tense now that I knew what to expect at the end of it. We parked in the same spot and Mama anxiously kissed me on the head before leaving the car. I watched her red ponytail sway as she made her way down the row of headstones to the bench, and again she sat there alone as two o'clock came and went.

What was she thinking as she waited for the hungry thing to come? She must have loved him once… and then to learn the terrible truth about him, to flee it all these years – to know she'd always carry a piece of his horror within her, because of *me*—

I tensed as the eerie figure again scurried out of the trees surrounding the cemetery. It was ridiculous to imagine this creature doing something so mundane as catching a bus, so either my father lived here – a fitting lair for a monster – or else he snuck here through shadows and dark places… and if so, where else might be within his reach?

My father seemed further devoured by his own hunger, scrawnier and more on edge than the year before. He looked vaguely like a Tim Burton creation from a distance—Mama and I loved *The Nightmare Before Christmas* and watched it every December—but there was nothing whimsical about him as he sat beside Mama. She handed him the envelope and he disembowelled it as if digging for a raw and bloody treat. He stared at my picture for long seconds, then tucked it into his coat. He looked around to ensure there were no witnesses, and the pale oval of his face turned toward the car.

I flinched and sank down in my seat, but too late. The monster leaped to its feet, and before Mama could do more than cry out in protest, it was hurtling down the path between headstones toward me. It grew closer and clearer by the second, and I couldn't tear my eyes away. The creature was so dreadful that I was held hypnotised. I heard a beep and a clunk – Mama using her key fob to lock the car from a distance, and not a moment too soon. For then my father was throwing himself against the car window and staring hungrily in at me.

He was the most horrid thing I had ever seen. His hair stuck up in wild clumps, his black clothes were dirty, and I could smell stale sweat and fresh desperation through the door seals. His hands spread themselves on the window like eager spiders, and his *face*—to this day, it haunts my dreams. His cheeks were sallow and unshaven, his eyes sunken and red-rimmed but so intent upon me they bulged out of his skull, and his cracked lips spread into a terrible grin. A pale, ugly tongue flicked out to moisten his hungry smile and I saw he'd lost some teeth, no doubt from splitting bones to get at their sweet marrow.

I screamed. He grinned and tried the door handle and placed his hands back on the glass like he could shatter it through will alone, and I screamed.

And then Mama was grabbing him by the

shoulders, pulling him away. She kicked and punched at him in a furious manner that suggested she knew violence all too well. My father cowered under her blows, but his ghastly eyes flared with rage, and I knew he was preparing to fling himself upon her. He'd savage Mama, find a way to get at me, and we'd both vanish into the gullet of this terrible ghoul.

Before he could spring, Mama reached into her jacket pocket and pulled out a piece of paper. It looked like a regular sheet of folded A4, nothing special. But she brandished it at my father like a Bible at a vampire.

"Remember this?" I heard her cry. "It still protects us. You know what will happen if I use it. So *get out of here!*"

My father scowled, and I couldn't believe those cruel lips had ever touched hers or shaped words of love. He was a wild beast, angry, *hungry*, and surely no mere piece of paper could hold him back. But he somehow brought his appetite under control, clenched his long-fingered hands into fists that remained down at his sides. He glanced at me, and for a moment he looked almost *ashamed*. Vibrating on the spot as if about to explode from frustrated hunger and violence, he turned and fled back down the path. By the time Mama had unlocked the doors and slipped into the driver's seat, my father was disappearing into the trees at the edge of the cemetery.

"Oh, honey!" She drew me into a protective embrace. "Are you okay?"

I nodded, wild with emotions I had no idea how to express.

"What is that? The piece of paper?"

Mama tucked it into her pocket as if caught with something foolish. "Oh…

some magic words. They keep him away. Let's go home, okay?"

Fine, but that house was not to be *home* much longer. Our packed belongings reminded me we were still on the run, as apart from the world as *him*. Mama said we could talk if I wanted, but I preferred to go alone to my room and try to digest this dreadful day. It lingered deep in my belly, and from that night, it repeated on me like the worst case of heartburn you can imagine.

Father lurked and leaped in my dreams. Sometimes he looked as he had in the cemetery, frightful and voracious; other times, even worse. Sometimes he had devolved further into a misshapen monstrosity, a drooling Gollum driven insane by need. But always he knew me, and wanted me, and came for me. And I didn't always wake up before he caught me.

I remained vigilant in our new house, sure that he was creeping through our garden by night, watching, waiting for his chance to strike. Perhaps he was biding his time until I ripened, became more tasty— or more like *him*. That thought was the worst, and I did everything in my power to prevent it. I caught Mama's anxious eyes when I went for seconds at dinner and changed my mind; in time, I was eating as little as I possibly could. When the ache in my belly grew too fierce from lack of food, I munched on seeds, grass, bits of paper, anything bland to fill the hole and stop it growing ever deeper.

Mama fretted, but I wouldn't listen and stayed my course. She loved me and provided what help she could, her smiles becoming ever smaller and sadder as she watched me fight my appetite. It occurred to me that although my father had failed to devour me, he'd swallowed my childhood nonetheless. He'd eaten everything that made me happy, everything good, all that I thought was *me*.

I told myself I would never be like him. And inside me all the while, denied and deprived, my hunger grew.

***

My eleventh birthday was the second time I'd had my Polaroid taken with full knowledge of its destination. This time I didn't even try to smile, and Mama gave up trying to coax me into it.

"I really don't think you should come today. Not after last year. He'll be looking for you."

"So? You've still got your magic words, don't you?"

Mama frowned and nodded, though she must have noted my scepticism. Magic words, *really*? Did she think I was a baby? That paper had looked just like a regular document—it wasn't even in Latin. I suspected it was a mere prop that she'd used to bluff my father, and while I respected the ingenuity, I felt insulted by her insistence it was enchanted.

"Why do you still want to come? After all the nightmares, honey—why?"

I had been practicing my response for weeks.

"I want to tell him it doesn't matter that I'm his son—I'm not going to turn out rotten and hungry like him. I know it's about genetics and stuff I don't understand, but I won't do it, Mama. *I will not be a monster.*"

"No, sweetie." She folded me into her soothing embrace, that sense of yielding and unyielding both that defines motherhood. "You won't. I'll make sure of

it."

I carried that promise on the drive to the cemetery, clutched at it as desperately and hopelessly as I would the rays of sunlight that lit upon us. Fear harrowed me, but I didn't hide as Mama walked through the stones and took her seat on the bench. My father would surely know I was here— maybe he'd be able to *sense* me now, smell the hunger and corruption growing in me with each passing year. I sat up straight and waited for him to creep out of the trees, ready to defy him.

But no thin, wasted figure slunk from the shadows this year. Instead, a portly old lady walked out of the maze of graves, hesitated, then sat down beside Mama. I cursed, sure this woman would scare my father away—or that I'd have to watch him eat her—but Mama engaged her in conversation. Wasn't she worried that the deal was broken, that the hunger would be unleashed upon us?

Evidently not. Her shoulders slumped as though a weight had lifted from her, and then she shocked me by passing the stranger my latest Polaroid. The old woman laid one hand on Mama's shoulder before rising and leaving the bench.

Mama must have told her about me, because the lady walked down toward our car, and she was looking at me all the way. I watched her closely in case this was a trick—maybe my father had taken on a new form, a concept so obvious I couldn't believe I'd never thought of it, or maybe she was in thrall to his evil and would try to snatch me. But instead she met my gaze, paused on the path, and sent me a slow, sad smile. There was no hunger in it—an emptiness that yearned to be filled, yes, but no appetite. I tentatively waved, and she waved back, touching a handkerchief to her shimmering eyes before disappearing into the forest of stones.

Mama returned to the car a few minutes later, her make-up smudged by tears.

"What's happening? Who was that lady? Why are you crying?"

"Turns out that… was your grandmother. *His* mum."

She sat for a moment, trembling hands braced on the steering wheel, then turned to me with solemn, shining eyes.

"Honey… your father is dead."

The words stunned me into a statue. Of course, *that* was why she was crying—such relief! To be free of the creature's curse at last, to finally stop running and live in peace… she must have felt so *happy*.

"But… how? I mean, how do you even kill a monster? Was it bullets? Silver? Fire?"

Mama shook her head, eyes squeezed closed as if she'd been dealt a deep wound.

"It was *ice*," she said.

This made no sense to me at all. Was my father frozen solid? Crushed beneath an avalanche? I tried to ask, but Mama shushed me, her face wet and drawn, and started the car.

I said just one more thing on the drive home.

"I guess we don't need the magic words anymore."

"Oh, kiddo." She sighed as if I still believed that silliness. "That was a restraining order—and a fake one, at that. I couldn't go to the police… too many questions."

Mama wanted to be alone in her room that afternoon. It seemed weird to me, mourning a monster, but I reminded myself she had loved him once, back when

she'd thought he was human. And even though I didn't resemble him at all, it had to have been hard for her to look at me every day and remember. I let her be and gamed until she emerged to fetch us a pizza for dinner.

"I'm sorry you're sad," I said, breaking the cheesy strings that bound my next slice to the rest. "But things will be better now the monster's dead."

Mama dropped her pizza fast as if angered, but her eyes were sad—even a little guilty.

"We're not going to call him that anymore, okay? Your father turned bad, but he wasn't *evil*. He was just… weak. An addict."

"But you said—"

"I know, kiddo. But sometimes you say things, like… well, Father Christmas, the Tooth Fairy, that sort of thing… and then later, you have to take them back. I know you're confused, sweetie. I'll explain it all someday—there's a lot you need to know. But tonight, just let Mama get on with her work, and tomorrow we'll settle in our new place, and one day… I'll tell you about your father. About me and you."

I frowned and dropped the subject. Why was she letting him off the hook? A dead monster was still a monster, right? But apparently my father had been innocent once – infected with some disease, finally finding freedom in death.

I went back to gaming after dinner while Mama grabbed her bag of tools and headed out. She looked exhausted when she returned, as though she'd faced a tremendous personal test and wasn't sure whether she'd passed or failed.

"It's all done, kiddo. Come have your nightcap."

Great – my least favourite part of the birthday ritual. I joined Mama at the kitchen table, and, as always, a plastic jug sat before me, another before her. It was gross, but she made me drink the whole thing. The red stuff was thick and still a little warm, the taste uncomfortably familiar—like something I'd had in my mouth before, when a tooth fell out or I ate too much chocolate. It couldn't be *that*, I told myself, but things were starting to come together in the back of my mind, and it made an awful kind of sense.

My birthday nights were always strenuous because of all the change, and I didn't sleep any better this time. But I made it through, and when I woke in the morning, Mama was waiting beside my bed.

As always, it took me a few seconds to process the sight and understand this stranger was my mother. She had long honey-blonde hair now and her face was rounder, fuller. She wore glasses and was six inches taller than last night. But I saw Mama in her eyes, and knew I'd quickly grow accustomed to her new appearance.

And mine.

"Good morning, baby. Guess what your name is now!"

I didn't get it – I never did. I repeated the new syllables to myself all day, getting used to them, making them second nature. We packed our boxes into the old car and drove to our new house, which still smelled of disinfectant from Mama's visit last night. I ran around and explored while she scrubbed at a couple of dark stains she'd missed.

Everything went on much the same as before. We kept to ourselves, even when people came by and said they knew us; they always looked confused and upset when they left. Mama taught me my words and numbers at home and sometimes she'd take me out, but not too often, not too openly. Our year as this blonde Mama and son played out like all those before, right down to our birthday ritual on moving day as I turned twelve.

Once more, Mama stood me against the loungeroom wall and took two Polaroids. As we shook them to aid the emulsion, I asked why she still needed two photos, since my father would no longer be needing one. Mama regarded me sadly for a long moment, put one picture aside, and stroked the other with gentle fingers.

"The promise still stands, kiddo," she said. "This one is for his grave."

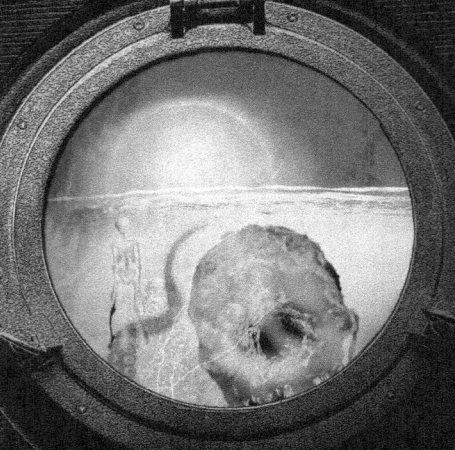

THE
**AUSTRALIAN HORROR
WRITERS ASSOCIATION**
PRESENTS

In Sunshine Bright & Darkness Deep
AN ANTHOLOGY OF AUSTRALIAN HORROR

ON SALE
NOW

HELL'S BELLS

STORIES OF
FESTIVE FEAR
BY MEMBERS OF
THE AUSTRALIAN
HORROR WRITERS
ASSOCIATION

AHWA
australianhorror.com

THE LIGHTHOUSE
BY CLAIRE FITZPATRICK

Veronica pulled the plate of pancakes from the microwave. She'd reheated them three times, twice forgotten. She fetched the jam from the cupboard and a butter knife from the drawer, then ventured outside to the weathered cast-iron table and chairs on the first landing of the zig-zagged wooden staircase leading down to the beach. Slowly, robotically, miserably, she ate.

Veronica gazed up at the lighthouse. While the original wooden structure had living quarters attached, over time, the house fell into dilapidation, and was eventually demolished after a furious storm knocked out three of the four walls. Later, the entire lighthouse had been rebuilt out of whitewashed reinforced concrete, with added floors for living areas. Ben had marvelled at the 'unique quirkiness' of living in a lighthouse. Veronica had been hesitant.

She pursed her lips. She didn't like the circular windows. Usually, she thought they added a unique touch to the architecture or geometry of a building, but on this lighthouse, they seemed to peer at her, like eyes in a painting following her as she passed. And she didn't like the stairs inside. Ostensibly winding, she tripped every time she walked upon them; some days her feet seemed too big, and she'd have to pause and grip the railing in fear of falling. Ben laughed it off as all in her head. She was nervous about the pregnancy, and the massive changes in her life.

She sighed. He was right. He always was.

Everything would be fine.

***

"Wake up, baby. Come on, play with me!"

The duty obstetrician smiled as the sonographer smeared cold gel on Veronica's stomach and began moving the probe. A long, silent moment passed. And then another. And then her silence was too long, and Veronica's heart sank.

"Is she…. not OK?"

The sonographer bit down on her bottom lip. "She's being a bit tricky today."

The room was quiet for another few moments. The sonographer and the obstetrician exchanged a concerned look.

"I'm so sorry."

"But she was kicking and rolling last night. What are you saying?"

The obstetrician's face was pale. "Love, she's passed away."

"But…. what did I do wrong?"

"Nothing. We'll check for infections, but just know these things happen."

"But where does she go?"

The woman took a deep breath. "You give birth to her."

"But she's…. not alive."

"We induce the labour, and after she's born you can spend time with her until it's time to take her away."

"What do you mean?"

"Well, you can dress her-we can make impressions of her hands and feet. Maybe take a lock of her hair? We can take photos of her."

"Like those Victorian freaks?"

"No, no, not like that. You create a memory of her. You're still her parents.

She's still your baby."

Afterwards, Ben placed her in a Moses basket and carried her to the hospital chapel to be blessed. Only then did Veronica allow herself to cry.

***

The butter knife was cold on her tongue as Veronica licked away the last of the jam. She threw it down the stairs and it landed in the sand. Sighing, she stood and walked over to retrieve it, then turned to face the lighthouse.

Ben appeared at the top of the staircase. "Are you OK, V?"

Veronica frowned. "I only just sat down."

Ben frowned and looked down at his watch. "It's ten-thirty, hon. You've been out here for hours."

Ben walked down the staircase and they sat at the table in silence, gazing out across the water.

Veronica sighed. "Doesn't she speak to you?"

"Who?"

"You know who."

"I told you 'no' before." He bit down on his bottom lip. "What does she say?"

Veronica wrinkled her nose. "She says she's trapped. Alone."

"Maybe it's your subconscious? And she's voicing your fears of feeling trapped in a cycle of childlessness."

"Maybe."

They were silent for a few moments, until Ben cleared his throat. "Weird question, but how come you've been leaving all the doors open?"

Veronica frowned. "What do you mean?"

"All the doors. It's cold and draughty in the staircase. Keep them shut."

"I didn't open them."

Ben looked at her and bit his bottom lip.

"OK."

***

The second pregnancy was easier. No morning sickness. No back pain. Veronica plucked up the courage to decorate the nursery, buying knitted baby blankets and an aquatic-themed mobile, with little fish, starfish, crabs, and turtles. She'd chatted about the pregnancy with Ben's clients at the barbershop, and imagined a world where they were happy, and their baby was healthy and thriving.

One blustery spring morning, she'd felt the urge to get out of the house for a walk, though it had taken her almost an hour to leave. Every time she'd move to put on her shoes, the smoke alarm would go off, pulling her back in. Behind the lighthouse stood a line of birch trees, dense and pointed like teeth in a mouth. Despite her fatigue, she'd followed the path to where the foliage grew weak and paused as it opened to a circle of stones with a small, rounded stone in the middle. Carved into the stone were dates. Three months. Six Months. Eight months.

Veronica pressed her hands into her pockets and looked out over the ocean. A gale blew off the headland, filling her nostrils, her lungs. She coughed, dropping to her knees, her windpipe saturated with too much air. For a split second, it seemed she was looking at herself from above, strapped to the wings of a seabird as it danced along with the wind. She saw not just herself but other women, other babies and her ears filled with the sound of infant cries, so loud she thought her eardrums would burst. Then it was over, and she was left panting on the ground, alone.

Later, Ben told her it was a panic attack. So, she'd led him to where the headstones were, only to find them gone. He suggested she'd fallen asleep. The pregnancy was more tiring than the last.

When she reached the eighth-month mark, Ben bought a baby bath, and it sat in the corner of the bathroom, waiting. The night before the due date, Veronica didn't sleep, despite drenching her pillow with lavender oil and taking melatonin, nothing she did would alleviate her stress. She'd laid there in the dark, listening to Ben's soft gentle snores.

Then came the blood.

The labour took place in abnormal silence. Veronica convinced herself she was asleep, and when it was over, she would wake with a wailing baby in her arms. But as soon as the baby was placed against her chest, Veronica knew she wasn't dreaming. This was real. Here was her baby–another baby–dead.

"Hello, my sweet angel," she'd whispered, pressing her warm lips to his cold forehead. "Hello."

Ben held their baby to his face, inhaling the scent of him.

"It's me–my body!" Veronica had exclaimed between sobs on their way home.

Ben's knuckles were white on the steering wheel. "It's not you, V."

"Two babies, Ben! *Two!* It hurts so much. My arms don't know what to do. They should be cradling a baby. But all they cradle is death!"

When they'd returned to the lighthouse, Ben jumped in the shower, but Veronica remained in the car, staring at the white monolith, a guardian of the ocean, but a foe to her womb. Maybe Ben was right? Maybe it wasn't her after all?

***

Veronica returned to the kitchen and filled the kettle, rummaging for tea bags in the crumpled box. The following two miscarriages occurred in the first trimester and seemed like nothing more than a heavy period. But the third was hell. At nineteen weeks, Veronica was in the shower when she began to bleed. At the hospital, the nurse gave her three glasses of water and told her to prepare for an ultrasound. An hour later, she gave birth to a baby without a face.

Veronica carried her tea upstairs to the bedroom, each step an effort. Despite being reasonably fit, it felt as though she carried the weight of several babies. Her steps were sluggish, legs almost tripping over themselves. When she reached the bedroom, she collapsed onto the bed, exhausted.

After she'd moved in, Ben threw himself into the renovations, drawing up his plans for his home barbershop. The spiral staircase boasted ninety-five stairs between eight floors–a kitchen, two living areas, a bathroom, two bedrooms, and a library–leading to the lantern room at the top of the tower, with a polished copper-domed roof. Each had granite floors and whitewashed walls, the bathroom with an overpriced French cast-iron roll-top bath. But Ben insisted. This was their home–everything had to be perfect for the family they would one day have.

"Do you think the nursery is the wrong colour?"

Veronica rolled over in bed and pulled the blankets over her face. "It's not the colour, Ben. It's this house. And those stairs."

Ben poked her shoulder. "You know it's all in your head, right?"

She peered out from under the blankets. "Just because it's in my head doesn't mean it's not true."

"Well, what do you mean? Mould?"

Veronica shrugged. "I don't know. It's just…do you remember when we went on the cruise, and it took you much longer than anyone else to get your sea legs?"

"Yeah."

"It's like that. However, just when I'm about to put my foot on the last stair, it's like I'm stepping from the boat to the land, except I miss my footing and fall into the water."

Ben raised a brow. "A bit dramatic?"

"I just have a…a feeling, you know? Like maybe I'm not supposed to be here. Maybe I shouldn't have moved in. Does that make sense?"

Ben frowned. "So… you don't want to live with me?"

"Of course, I do! Oh… I don't know."

"OK. Well, how about burnt sienna? For the paint?"

"That's a hair colour, Ben."

"Copper?"

"Hair colour."

"You want me to leave it blue?"

Veronica groaned. "I thought it was cerulean blue?"

"Idiot."

Ben left to see his apprentice at the barbershop, and she listened to his footsteps as he descended the tower, around and around, until he reached the kitchen and they stopped. She wished he believed her. At least then she could yell and scream and vent some of her frustration and it would be OK.

Veronica rolled onto her side. She would have to return to work, but all she wanted to do was shut out the world. She closed her eyes, and then she felt it-a hot, moist exhale against her face, struggling to breathe through a jagged windpipe-followed by the soft coos of an infant.

"Ben!"

Bolting upright, she sprinted from the room, racing downstairs, hands clenched on the railings. She was halfway when a gust of wind blew into her, blundering, racing. She flattened herself against the stone wall for balance, heart hammering in her chest as she imagined falling down the stairs to her death. Her fingers dug so hard into the whitewashed brick walls her nails chipped. She was about to scream when the wind passed, and she stepped back from the wall, hands shaking, a shrill, agonised cry for help tumbling around her mind.

She pressed a hand to her heart. It wasn't her voice.

***

The day dragged on, the afternoon arriving on the coattails of a storm. Ben arrived home in good spirits. Despite desperately relaying to him what happened, once again, Ben assumed it was all in her head. He'd ducked out to go to the shops, promising to be back in an hour. But Veronica knew he wouldn't be back until dark, smelling of scotch. As each pregnancy failed, he'd stayed out longer and longer. Veronica ascended the ladder to the lantern room and climbed through the hatch, wondering if there would come a day he wouldn't return.

The lantern room was the most beautiful place in the lighthouse, with wide windows and a little door leading to a cast-iron circular observation deck with metal stanchions supporting a horizontal guardrail. Ben intended to turn it into a library room and boxes of books sat unattended against the walls. Cushions and blankets and old newspapers sat heaped together atop a large brown canvas travelling trunk.

Veronica walked to one of the windows and looked out to the sea. The waves rolled inwards, blue-green as they pulsed against the shore in a steady, rhythmic beat. Silver clouds gathered in the sky, swirling in steady, radiating ripples. For a split second, she imagined filling her clothes with weights and throwing herself into the water, sinking to the shadowy depths below. She pressed her forehead against the window and closed her eyes.

The fourth and fifth babies were ectopic twins. As soon as the doctor told her the embryos were in her fallopian tube, Veronica almost fainted. Two weeks later, her tubes ruptured, and she was rushed into surgery with internal bleeding. Ben's hand was warm in hers as she lay in the hospital bed, staring at the ceiling.

"My babies are trying to kill me, Ben."

He'd squeezed her hand. "This happens, V. It's normal."

"*Normal?* I almost bled to death!"

"I know, but you didn't. You're alright."

"Six, Ben! Six ghosts haunt me!"

She'd spent a week in hospital as doctors ran tests on her immune cells to determine if they were the root of her problems. Veronica heard whispers of 'killer cells', but at the end of the week, they had no definitive answers. Her obstetrician suggested they should speak to a therapist, either together or alone. Veronica declined. She stayed in bed, skipped showers, ignored her aching breasts, and cried.

Veronica opened her eyes and stepped away from the window, looking around the room.

"Why do you want my babies?" she hissed.

Tears rolled down her cheeks as she tugged at the ends of her hair, stomach churning.

After the first stillborn, a grief counsellor told her it took strength to be miserable in a world of beauty, blessings, and benevolence. But she disagreed. Hope was a contract entered by fools.

Sighing, she lay on the floor, staring at a cluster of spiders as they scurried across the domed ceiling, their movements methodical and timed, as though following a rhythmic beat. They reached a large web tucked in the joint where the ceiling met the wall and noticed two fat spiders, one with an engorged abdomen. Veronica rolled her eyes and retrieved a cold tea bag from a cup, throwing it at the pregnant spider. It scurried across the web to its mate. She glared at them, jealousy twisting in her stomach with the ferocity of a knife.

Then she heard a cry. It was quiet at first and she'd almost mistaken it for the whistling and whoosh of the wind, but this was different. It was high-pitched and rhythmic, repetitive, and distressed. Veronica dry-swallowed. The cries belonged to a new-born gulping in air between sobs. Heart hammering, she stood, listening to the cries as they reverberated around the room.

Ben. He'd likely finished shopping by now, having a pint at the village pub. Veronica frowned. Maybe it would be good to get out of the house? There were still a few hours until sunset, and if Ben *was* at the pub, they could have a meal and get back in time before it got too dark. He'd appreciate a hand carrying the shopping in, anyway.

The cries became more urgent, like colic, and she paced the room, trying to pinpoint their location, but they were everywhere and nowhere.

"Shut up!" She snapped, trying to block out the cries. "*Shut up, shut up, shut up!*"

And then….quietude. Solace.

A crack of thunder split the silence. Veronica glanced out the wide windows. She chewed the inside of her cheek, brows furrowed. When had it grown so dark? Stars speckled the sky like spilt sugar over black marble, singing infinite patterns. She wondered what the original lighthouse keeper saw when they looked at the sky. An endless void as she did? She looked at the chest once more, then went downstairs, searching for her car keys.

***

Despite the rumbling sky, the pub was rowdy, filled with locals, ruddy cheeks, wide smiles, and slaps on the back, the perfume of beer and rum permeating the air. Patrons wove around tables like smoke. Two people played a game of pool inside. Smokers sat on stools in the courtyard, warmed by towering patio heaters. Veronica hesitated before heading inside, eyes scanning the crowd for Ben, but she couldn't see him anywhere.

She made the rounds, asking everyone what they knew about the lighthouse. Everyone had a different story, though insistent on their truth.

A baby died there from SIDS.

A mother smothered her baby.

She fell from the observation deck holding the baby.

She jumped with the baby in her arms.

The father smothered the baby and pushed the mother down the beach staircase.

Veronica learned the grim tales had become a bit of an urban legend. Frustrated, she leaned against the lattice courtyard wall, arms crossed, looking down at her bare feet.

"Why are you doing this?"

Veronica jumped.

Ben stood in front of her, one hand on his hip, the other holding a half-empty glass of beer. He stared at her for a few moments, then placed the beer on an empty table, gripped her by the shoulders, and steered her away from the crowd.

"You've got to stop." His eyes were gentle, yet his tone was stern. "I'm trying to make friends. Trying to get clients for when I open the shop. You're going to scare them off."

"You heard them! It wasn't in my head!"

"People dying in a lighthouse has nothing to do with your pregnancy issues. It's not fucking haunted! I know you're opening all the doors to convince me otherwise, but it's not working."

"Are you kidding? It's not me. *I'm* not the problem. It's the house! It doesn't want me here!"

"But you are the problem, V! All this stuff," he waved his hands about. "It's you!"

"You're blaming *me?* It pushed me down the stairwell! I could have died!"

Ben sighed. "I'm not saying it's your fault, but maybe your body can't handle it? Maybe the stress is getting to you?"

"It's not! The stone circle, the graves–"

"There was nothing there, V."

"What do you mean? You saw them!"

Ben raised his brows. "I went to where you said they were and there was nothing there."

"They *are* there! I bet you didn't even look because you don't care!"

"*How can you say that?*"

Veronica tugged on the ends of her hair. "Everything was fine before we moved here! Why are you so blasé about it all? And why would all these people tell me about all the terrible things that happened in the lighthouse if it didn't mean something? And why would I hear their cries?"

"What cries?"

"The babies' cries!"

"Enough!"

The slap was quick and hard, leaving a bright red mark across her cheek. Veronica gaped at Ben, his shocked face mirroring her own.

'V, I'm sorry, I didn't mean–"

Turning on her heel, she stormed out of the pub, hurrying over to her car and climbing in. The key was in the ignition before she realised she'd retrieved it from her handbag. Only once the car park was far behind her was she able to take a steady breath. She hadn't expected him to strike her in front of such a large crowd. He'd never done it before. But he was wrong. So wrong. It wasn't all in her head. It wasn't.

***

Veronica placed her empty glass of wine on the sink and glanced at her laptop open on the kitchen table. Post-partum psychosis. *Most women with postpartum psychosis will experience psychosis (a 'psychotic episode') and other symptoms very soon after giving birth, usually within the first two weeks…. Symptoms can include hallucinations, delusions, a manic mood, a low mood, a mixture of both low and manic, feeling suspicious or fearful, restless…. not sure what causes postpartum psychosis…*

She'd watched documentaries about women experiencing postpartum psychosis before, however, none of them had reported feeling haunted by their house. Even that seemed delusional to her. Sighing, Veronica walked over to the table, closed her laptop, and sat down. She rubbed her eyes. For a split second, it seemed as though she was looking at the room through a glass of water. The edges of the room curved, like there were too many angles for her to settle on. The light fractured and reflected around the room and within the refracted light she saw a face. Startled, she jumped, knocking the glass to the ground. The front door handle jiggled, turned, and opened. Veronica moved towards it only to have it slam shut, like an angry slap across the face. A cold drowsiness overcame her as a warm trickle of blood rolled down her nose, and she found herself climbing the staircase with an unfamiliar gait, unbalanced and uncontrollable. No matter how loudly she commanded her legs to stop they carried on. She dug her nails into the walls, though they were of no use. Three of them ripped off altogether, leaving behind bloodied streaks on the walls. Her body thrust itself forward, round and round, up, up, up the stairs to the lantern room. And then the door slammed shut behind her and she was alone.

***

Veronica stood on the observation deck, arms crossed, and stared out across the water, watching the waves lap against the shore, the thin sea-mist settling over the rockpools. It was dark, after midnight, and still Ben had not come home. She began to pace and circled the deck. No matter how many times she'd wrestled with the door handle, she hadn't been able to leave the lantern room. The lighthouse wanted her here.

Veronica leaned over the railing, drawing in a deep breath of the cool night air blowing in from the wispy sea. She looked down. Amongst the tidewrack and seafoam, crustacean shells and feathers were babies. She covered her mouth to catch her breath and stared at their tiny bodies washing up on the shore. She thought of the haunting words of the patrons at the pub. *The baby died from SIDS. The mother smothered the baby. The mother fell from the observation deck holding the baby. She jumped with the baby in her arms. The father smothered the baby and pushed the mother off the observation deck. He poisoned them all and killed himself afterwards.* As she looked upon the bodies, she heard their plaintive, piercing, and incessant cries. The sound drifted in and out of her ears, and she felt it resonate within, wrapping itself around her, strangling her bones.

"*Wake up, baby. Come on, play with me!*"

Veronica jumped at the voice, dread gnawing her insides as she pictured the day in the hospital and the moment she knew she'd never feel her baby's heartbeat against her own. She stared at the little bodies on the beach, face down as they swallowed sand. She gasped as they rolled over to look at her, their little eyes pleading for life. Her heart sank as the sand shifted and swallowed the infants, the tide coming in to wash all the remnants away.

She gripped the railing so hard her knuckles burned. "*Why are you doing this to me?*"

Her voice was an indignant roar, hysterical, angry, savage.

She wanted the freedom to grieve and move on. The grief counsellor at the hospital after her second stillborn told her and Ben they would heal, over time, even if it didn't seem they were healing at all. But the waiting to heal only unstitched her wounds, plunging her into darkness, into dreams where she felt helpless as a jellyfish, insubstantial, flung everywhere and nowhere by the hands of a cruel and merciless god.

She gazed across the land, until she saw it. The stone circle! She rubbed her eyes hard and when she opened them, it, and the babies, were gone.

The door swung open.

***

The cold crept and pinched at Veronica as she pulled off her nightgown and stepped into the warm bath. Ben had arrived home tipsy the night before, eager to make love. At first, she'd considered it. But then he'd seen her bloodied nails, bruised body, and confronted her. Of course, he hadn't believed a thing. She was cracking up–she was the one who'd pulled off her nails and smeared blood on the walls. *She* was losing it. It was a cry for attention. He'd found her laptop open and read through the characteristics of post-partum psychosis. In his mind, it all fit, and the only thing haunting her was herself.

She sank lower into the warm water and closed her eyes. Though the water sloshed a little as she moved, the momentum picked up and began to sway, jolting from one side of the bath to the other, as though the floor rocked beneath her. Heart thumping, she sat up to climb out of the bath, yet the force of the water held her down and pushed her under. She stared at the ceiling through the thin film of water, craving breath so desperately the need made her feel heavier than she'd ever felt before. The light above seemed far away. Her wilful limbs began to beat and flap about, and it seemed to Veronica strange colours and radiances were inside her brain, flashing faster and faster, until she was falling down the vast and interminable stairway of the lighthouse, round and round, the corpses of infants falling through the air, their cries ringing out around her. When she reached the bottom she fell into the gaping mouth of the lighthouse and it swallowed her whole.

"*Veronica!*"

Veronica gasped as Ben pulled her from the bath, wrapping his warm arms around her cold and soaking body. He reached for the heavy fleece towel on the rack and cocooned her with it, rubbing her shoulders and kissing her neck.

"I have to get out of here, Ben!" she spluttered. "The babies… they're going to keep dying."

"They won't. V. It'll happen, I promise. Please, you're not thinking straight."

"The house… it pulled me upstairs! It was like I was a puppet!"

Ben inhaled sharply. "V… you need help. I've rung the hospital and they recommended a psychiatrist for you. I booked an appointment for next week. You need a rest."

Veronica looked up, seeing her face reflected in Ben's troubled eyes. "Why don't you believe me?"

"V…." Ben hesitated. "After we lost the twins, I started talking to someone. By myself. I didn't tell you because I was

embarrassed. Seems dumb now. But it was helpful to talk about your pregnancies. I want to be a father just as much as you want to be a mother."

"But I *am* a mother," Veronica rasped. "A mother to death. And it's because of this house! It was like someone else controlled my legs! It forced me up the stairs so I could see all those dead babies!"

Tears welled in Ben's eyes. "I can't do this anymore."

He let go of her and left the bathroom. She listened to his hurried footsteps as he descended the staircase, the slam of the front door, and the crunching of the gravel as he drove away. She knew, this time, he wouldn't be back. But she didn't cry, she had no tears left to shed.

***

Ben wiggled his toes in the sand as the lacy blue-green water rolled across his feet. The cool breeze coated his skin in a thin layer of brine, and he inhaled the salt, tasting it on his tongue. To his left, a line of jellyfish left trails of lacy white ribbons, to his right, the driftwood eddied and knocked against one another in greeting. Above, stars lit the sky like snowflakes and a guttural squawk of a night heron shook a gathering of puffins from their nest.

Ben watched the ocean drift in and out. And then he heard it—the high-pitched distressing cry of a new-born. Frowning, he looked along the beach, realised he was alone. The cries grew louder, insistent, desperate, and Ben spun on his heels, eyes flickering in every direction. Then he looked up at the lighthouse.

The structure stood resolute, its round eyes staring at him, daring him to challenge its grip on his wife. It seemed to lean to one side, the windows were smaller than they should be and appeared to be staring right at him, like a spider with its multitude of eyes. He rubbed his own eyes and saw Veronica on the observation deck, leaning against the guardrail. He could see her outline and the flapping of her nightdress in the slight wind. He called out to her, yet she made no indication she heard him.

"Veronica! Go back inside!"

He bolted up the stairs and towards the lighthouse, legs carrying him as fast as they could, eyes firm on Veronica. When he reached the car, he froze.

Veronica climbed over the guardrail.

Ben held his breath.

The Daily U

Monday, May 15, 2022

Grim Discovery In Lighthou

Realtors were shocked to discover several mummified infants in an antique travelling trunk after inspecting a recently repossessed lighthouse.

Joan Dawson told police she and an evaluator had visited the lighthouse to determine suitability to be tenanted.

"There were several of them wrapped up in pink fleece," Ms Dawson said. "They had skin, hair...it was

shocking."

Police revealed the former occupants were a married couple in their early 30s, who resided at the property for three years before it was abandoned. Locals described the man as 'friendly' and the woman as 'fairly reclusive'.

The woman was reported to have taken her own life in the lighthouse. The man could not be reached for comment.

THE TUB
BY J. ASHLEY-SMITH

We found the tub in the wastes out back of the Kwik Fit tyre place. A dark overgrown no-man's-land of dirt and weeds between the back gardens and spiked fences of Richmond Road, and the mountains of bare, burst or burnt-out tyres in the Kwik Fit yard. Ivy, crab apple and cow parsley grew wild in that narrow space, unowned and shut off from the world. But me and Dave knew a way in—a secret way—down in the corner of the neighbourhood recreation ground.

We was bored and summer-holiday aimless, hungry for distraction. Some kid in Dave's class swore blind his brother found a stash of *Reader's Wives* in a Tesco's bag somewhere off the rec. So, we was sort of on a quest for porno mags, but also not really—just happy to be out of the house, in the sun, with purpose enough to make an adventure of it. We'd skirted the bushes behind the little-kid's playground, climbed the spiked iron railings and trampled the clumps of bramble and stingers what grew up against the tyre yard's high tin fence. There, at the corner, was a sheet of tin curled up at the edge. Under this we'd crawled into the dank wonderland beyond, that shady in-between place with its weird smell of creosote and compost, of sunshine and rubber. From one side, blackbirds and Radio 4. From the other, workshop clangour and the distant hum of main-road traffic. We didn't find no porno. What we found was the tub.

It was one of them old-fashioned bathtubs, with feet like a lion. The legs was ornate, clawed paws wrapped round with snakes. The base was ringed with designs: grape bunches, vine leaves and the like. White enamel it was—or *were*. It was so dingy with grime you couldn't imagine it'd ever truly gleamed. It lay askew, one lion's paw inches off the ground, the other corner sunk in dirt. Ivy'd grown all over and through, tangled between the legs and half covering one side. Must've been there an age.

The tub was nothing compared to what was inside. There must've been filth and leaves and all kinds of shit dropping in there for years. Whatever it was in there'd been decaying so long it turned to sludge, a foul black slurry so shiny and thick it looked like oil, like melted black rubber from all them tyres. And it *stank*. Godalmighty! You never smelled nothing like it: like chip-shop grease traps and the fishmonger's bins, and something worse than all the turds in the world just stacked up and left to rot.

"Mate!" I said and pulled back from the tub, eyes watering, nose covered with the crook of my elbow.

But Dave was right in there. He'd found a stick and was giving that festering muck a poke. It rippled, sluggish and slow, like its movements was bound by some other kind of time. The surface shimmered like puddles at the petrol station, wet blackness spangled with rainbows. A bubble rose and burst and out guffed a stench worse than the farts of our old dog, before we had to put him down.

"Really, geez," said Dave. "You could've waited."

"He who smelt it, dealt it."

"Whoever said the rhyme, did the crime."

This last Dave said automatically, his attention not on me nor the world around, but on the tub and what lay within. His face was a sight to behold, eyes wide with glee, mouth curled in disgust. He lifted the stick from the filth, the end glistening with dripping black goop. He leant in for a sniff and lurched, gagged. Went back for another. It was the same noise he made the night we snuck down the rec to drink Cabinet Cocktail, that godawful mix of every spirit in back of Mum's drinks cupboard. The cocktail was beyond foul, but that didn't stop Dave going back and back. And me following, as always. Then both of us spraying chunks in the shadow of the climbing frame. That look on his face, the noise he made—four parts revulsion, six parts curiosity—told me things was going to pan out just about as well.

"D'you bring your lunch?" he asked, pushing the stick back into the goo.

"No. What you on about?"

"S'alright," said Dave. "You can have some of mine." And he whipped out the stick and flicked it at me.

The filth missed me by an inch and I growled and dived at him. Then we was rolling about in the leaves, with me whacking at him hard as I could.

"Seriously though," said Dave as he pushed me off, fossicked in the ivy for another, longer stick. "This stuff is proper queer."

He poked the stick back in and swirled it around. The goo in the tub let out a slow, stinking bubble. Dave poked downward, right to the bottom. Only the stick didn't stop there—it just kept on going.

Expecting a floor but finding none, Dave stumbled, off balance. He grabbed the edge of the tub, caught himself just before he tumbled into the goop. The tub groaned beneath his weight.

The stick was right where Dave had left it, poking straight up out of the muck. But it was sinking, slow and certain, like in quicksand or a bog. Soon all what was left was six inches sticking out of that fatty black ooze, shimmering with sick-making rainbows.

I looked at Dave and he looked at me. Then we looked at the stick. I got down on hands and knees and peered beneath the tub. Down one side it was bogged, one leg and half the basin sunk under mud and leaves. But up the other end I could see clear through to the far side, to banks of moss festooned with ivy. And it was that end where the stick was sunk. It should've been out the underside and three foot in the ground. Only there wasn't no ground, just the grimy basin lifted six inches or more off the dirt, the claw foot raised like a lion on the prowl. And between the foot and the floor there was nothing. Just empty space.

Cautious as a thief, I slid my hand between, moved it this way and that. Nothing. Wherever the stick'd gone, it wasn't outside the tub.

Before we lost it to the goo, Dave grabbed it and gave it a tug. The bog'd got it, sucking and dragging from below.

"Giz a hand will you," he said. So, I went round the other side and helped him with the stick, pulling in a tug of war against the goop. Slowly, sickeningly, one, then two, then three and four feet of stick came out, with all but the end slick with black glop.

"Bloody hell," said Dave. But whatever

he was going to say next went unsaid, as someone yelled "Oi, you!" from one of the back gardens. Dave chucked the stick and we scarpered.

**

I didn't want to go back to the tub. I didn't like getting yelled at, didn't want no trouble for trespassing or whatnot. And the tub, with its slick of black goop what shimmered so queerly, gave me a wrong feeling. But when Dave came round next day, he was proper keen to get back there.

I tried to talk him out of it, thought maybe I could distract him with the new comics I'd bought, or a game of *Risk* or something. Or we could go to the library and look up the pictures of kids born wrong, or of grownups with their arms and legs all messed up from spider bites and the like. But all Dave wanted was to go back over the fence and into that shady no-place and look again at the tub and its filthy contents.

"I wanna try something," he said as we strolled the path down to the rec. It was a baking hot day and the fence was lined on either side with the white flowers of granny-pop-out-of-beds and the leavings of every dog in the neighbourhood. The little turd spirals had baked in the sun, turned chalky white as the flowers. I kicked one as we passed and it bounced ahead of us, burst into a cloud of white dust when it hit the fence.

Dave had brought his backpack with him, the one he used for school. Once we was over the railings and under the sheet of tin, he peeled open his bag and pulled something out, tossed it to me. It was heavy and round. A ball of glass with colours in it, like blue and yellow fireworks.

"What is it?"

"Paperweight, innit." Dave rummaged in the bag again and this time pulled out a reel of string. He gestured for the paperweight, began pulling out string, wrapping it round and around, this way and that, till it was proper secure. In the Kwik Fit yard, a forklift groaned, traffic murmured in the street beyond. Someone, somewhere was mowing the lawn. I was wigging out, looking over my shoulder for that bossy plonker who'd yelled at us last time.

"Here we go then," said Dave. "You ready?"

"For what?" I said. But Dave had already dropped the paperweight into the tub and was reeling out inches of string.

I looked inside. The goop had splashed up against the grimy porcelain and was oozing down, slow as you like. As Dave spooled out the string, it made cross shapes and stars in the muck. A bubble burst in slow motion on the surface.

"It don't make no sense," said Dave. The string on the spool was half gone, and still he turned it, reeling out more and more. Like he was flying a kite, only upside-down.

"What?"

"What d'you mean, 'What?' It's going down and down," said Dave. "But there in't nowhere for it to go to."

"Mate," I said. "That's not good."

The string was almost three-quarters unwound by now, still tight against the edge of the tub. Then suddenly it wasn't. The string went slack and Dave stumbled backwards, tripped over a stack of metal pickets, a roll of chain link from a fence never begun. Dripping black string slithered against the porcelain.

"Mate," I said again. "That's not right."

Dave picked up a small stick, then another, began to reel in the string, hand over hand, touching it only with the sticks. He didn't want to get none of that muck on his fingers. When he was done, there was a gooey black coil at his feet. Looped round and round, it made a biggish heap. There must've been thirty foot of it or more. The end of the string was all scraggly. The paperweight was gone.

"My dad's gonna give me a bollocking," said Dave as he poked around in the tub with one of the sticks. But it was useless. There was no way he'd find that paperweight in a tub with no bottom.

***

When he came round again next day, I didn't want none of it.

"Come on, Dave. Let's not. What d'you want with that stinking old tub anyway?"

"What are you—a baby? I never figured you for no chicken."

"I'm not chicken," I said. "It's just… wrong. No way it should go down deep as it does. It's messed up, Dave!"

"I know, right! I never seen nothing so messed up. Maybe there's nothing so messed up in all the world. And here it is, in your back garden almost. How can you *not* want another look?"

"I'm no chicken, but I am scared. Of it. Whatever's in there. Don't you wonder what broke the string?"

"You *are* a chicken," said Dave and he grabbed his backpack from the corner of my room. There was a sort of hollow scratching sound.

"What's in your bag?"

"Show you when we get there, won't I."

I wish now I'd never gone. Wish I'd ignored him, called his bluff. Just let him go… but then there we was, standing over that creepy old tub. The thick black sludge with rainbows shimmering.

Out of his bag Dave pulled a shoebox and a spool of garden twine. There was holes punched in the box lid. Something scratched inside. Dave reeled off a half-foot of twine and tied a slip knot. The he lifted the lid of the box from one corner and thrust in his hand. There was a mad scrabbling and Dave pulled out a rodent of some sort, white and chocolate-brown. Its tiny pink paws clawed at his fist.

"The fuck is that?"

"This," said Dave, "is Gilbert Grape. Or maybe… Edward Scatchy-paws? One of my sister's rats anyway. She'll never miss him." He slipped the knot over Gilbert-or-Edward's shoulders and pulled it snug. "And we'll have you back before she even knows you're gone, won't we?"

Cooing to the rat, Dave stooped over the tub.

"But what you gonna—"

He dropped it in the ooze.

Gilbert-or-Edward hit the goop with a splat. He thrashed wildly in that viscous sludge, twitching and writhing to keep his snout up, reeling from the stink. We stood watching as them little paws trod sluggishly in the black, the goo so thick the movements made no ripples, just a faint dip where his body sank slowly, slowly beneath the surface.

"Now what?" I asked, staring sort of sickened at the sharp little teeth, the pink little nose, the pitiful thrashing paws.

"It's not working," said Dave. "I figured he'd just sort of… sink. Here, you look for a rock or something and I'll—"

There was a groan from inside the tub. A deep metallic sound like the hull of a ship grinding against an iceberg. We both of us leaned in to see what was what.

A bubble the size of a fist broke the surface, then popped, splatting the grimy porcelain with a spray of black.

Gilbert-or-Edward's mad pawing went frenzied and he began to squeal. He was really moving now. He'd made it almost as far as the edge when the slithering thing broke the surface.

We both started yelling, me and Dave, all at once. "Fuck!" this and "Holy shit!" that, and "Did you fucking *see?!*" Thick as an arm it was and roundish, long and shiny like an eel, but sort of knobbled, lumpy like a tree branch. The whole thing was black as the pitchy goop in the tub and slick with the same ghastly iridescence. It surfaced again, oozing down in a sick-making slither. The black filth in the tub rippled ominously. Gilbert-or-Edward was yipping like mad. I thought he'd bring half the neighbourhood, it was so loud.

And then—just like that—it wasn't.

The head of the rat, bobbing at the surface, shrieking that dreadful shriek, just... wasn't there no more. All what was left was a crater in the goo, then a bubble slowly bursting. Then nothing. As if he'd never been.

Except for the twine now madly spooling.

What Dave should've done then was let go. Just drop the spool, drop it and run. We could've, both of us, been away from there—minus one rat, one paperweight, but otherwise none the worse. Only he didn't do that. When he felt the spool whirring in his hand, felt the twine sizzle through his fingers and down into the tub, he didn't let go like he should've. He gripped it tight, looped it in his fist.

I've played that moment over and over,

trying to figure it. Why? Why'd he *do* that? Why hold on, when fear and instinct and the sheer fucking madness of it all screams the opposite? Reflex, I suppose. He wasn't thinking, felt the spool twist and his hands just tightened round it. It was the worst thing he could've done.

The second his grip closed around the spool, the string pulled tight against the edge of the tub and Dave was yanked forward. There was a sickening *klunk* when his head hit the far side and a sort of dull plop as first his head, then head and shoulders, was dragged down into the filth. It was all over in seconds. One moment he was standing beside me, the next his feet was poking out of the black slop, kicking like mad. Then they too was gone and there was nothing. Just me and the tub and the dappled sun, faint breeze through the crab apple tree, the sound of blokes calling to each other from the tyre yard.

"Dave?" The word felt small in my throat, tiny in the still vastness of that summer afternoon. "Dave? Mate?"

My heart was tumbling. My ears rang, filling the silence from within. I took a step towards the tub.

Dave erupted from the surface with a gasp so loud I yelled. At least, I think it was Dave. Sticky black tar covered whatever it was. A head slick with filth, an open gasping mouth, and a hand reaching out to me.

"Help!" it gasped. "Help me!"

But I was shitting myself. I shrank away, tripped on a knot of ivy and fell backwards into the bushes.

The black-slick hand clamped onto the grimy white rim of the tub, gripping like mad. There was a sickening bubbling sound, then a long, drawn-out squeak, like someone dragging a squeegee down a window. The grip on the tub's edge weakened. The hand slipped from sight.

By the time I'd found my feet and scrambled back over, there wasn't even a ripple.

I didn't dare go no closer to that monstrous tub, but I couldn't leave Dave in there neither. I pushed at the toppermost edge. It hardly budged—little more than a wiggle. I looked around in the dirt and ivy for something I could use, snatched up one of the metal pickets from the unmade fence. I slid it beneath the tub's raised corner and lifted, using it like a lever.

That old tub was bastard heavy, heavy as you'd imagine cast iron and porcelain and a bottomless black lake might be. I strained against the picket, face twisted with the effort, the sharp edges cutting into my shoulder and hands. And I was yelling too, swearing at that fucking tub, shouting for Dave to let him know I was coming. I didn't care who heard me, didn't give two shits if Mr "Oi, you!" came back to give me a roasting. All I could think of was my mate in the tub. And just when I thought it was useless, just when I thought I was done and couldn't push no more, the tub groaned, lifted, tipped.

Then it was up and over and the black filth was sloshing all around, blorping out of that tub with a glopping sound like an upended bottle of ketchup.

It glopped and glopped, but still the black goop kept coming. It oozed through the fence into the tyre yard, down into the dry ditch along the backs of the Richmond Road gardens. It pooled round the old crab apple tree, what wobbled, leaned, then sank into the black.

It was coming so fast I had to back up. I didn't see Dave, nor Gilbert-or-Edward, nor the paperweight, nor none of that hundred yards of twine. There was only the goo slicking everywhere, glipping and glopping until that no-man's land, that in-between place, was all over black and I turned and ran. Back under the sheet of rusting tin, over the railings, past the climbing frame and the little-kids' swings and across the rec. By the time I reached the path, the black goop was seeping out and onto the playground.

***

When the phone rang that evening, I knew what was what. Mum asked if I'd seen Dave that day. And all I wanted was to be done with it, to tell her all and collapse in the flood of confusion and grief sloshing round inside of me. But all we'd been through, all we'd seen, was a lump in my throat so heavy and hard it was like a dam holding all of it back. Just an ache in my neck and a story too big to tell. I shook my head.

Dave hadn't been home. And only I knew he never would.

They've closed off the rec now and Richmond Road's under quarantine. There's red and white traffic fences up along the streets around. There's coppers and what looks like the army on guard. The Kwik Fit tyre shop's all dark and no one's seen the owners. A few of the lads who was working the yard haven't been seen neither. Everyone says the 'environmental disaster' had something to do with all them tyres. But it doesn't seem right to me.

I shower a lot these days, wash my hands every chance I get. But no matter how much I scrub and scrub, how much I lather the soap, I can't get rid of the smell.

Like grease-traps and fish-bins and all the turds in the world.

Mum's always saying what a clean boy I've become. But you won't catch me dead in no bath.

TEST OF DEATH
BY MICHAEL BOTUR
WINNER OF THE 2021 ROBERT N STEPHENSON SHORT STORY COMPETITION

My best friend doesn't wanna die, but his cancer is irreversible and the sky is black and booming so I'm swallowing three of his Tramadols with a nip of eighty-dollar cognac, back turned, hovering shamefaced over the armoire where Jarrod keeps his dusty trophies and awards and un-drunk alcohol. I'm a shitty nurse, I know. I don't know what else to do except stand around and take his possessions and watch him die. I'm his oldest friend. He tells me to do stuff, I do it for him. He tells me to give his suits to the St. Vincent de Paul. Okay, I'll do it. Give his Hot Wheels cars to my nephew. Throw out his trophies – fair enough, it's not as if I deserve one. I haven't done anything to slow his cancer. We're supposed to be high school teachers, supposed to act brave in front of 200 kids every week, but Jarrod is behind me, watching TV slumped on his side, melting into the couch, and I can't face him.

Because tumours are devouring his insides and he's told me to help myself to anything in the house—his drugs, booze, washer-dryer, vinyl collection and Star Wars figurines—I'm filling a laundry basket with precious things, heavy with shame. I throw in a letter opener, a scented candle, benzies, opioids, all his pills and die cast toys and rare albums, sniffling while I work. I've moved the washer-dryer into the laundry, along with a suitcase of Jarrod's shirts. I'll come back with a trailer and take the vinyl, though I'm scared of what'll happen after. Removing his possessions feels like pulling a plug out of a bathtub. The dregs of his life will swirl away. If I stop packing up his life, will it even slow the cancer? I don't know. People are coming round for a dinner party tonight everyone assumes will be his last. That's pretty final.

Jarrod is snapping his fingers at me from where he's splayed on the couch. The clicking thing is rude, though he gets a pass. Rudeness and gloomy sodden days are all we have. It's May 14 and the rains are coming every day and we don't expect him to last through the winter.

I creep back to the couch and hand him a glass of water and crushed up morphine tablets and a long circus straw which he can sip without adjusting his body.

Since he's sold his armchairs and his rug that he brought back from Egypt, I find a space for my butt on the couch edge. It's gross, having a dead man near – okay, he's not dead yet, it's just that Jarrod sees himself as nearly dead. Jarrod embraced his bowel cancer in February, expected to die by the end of March, and started getting mottled like mold-stained wallpaper in April. What hurts him now isn't the cramps or the beetroot-coloured poo or the burned skin. It's the uncertainty, the pointlessness of his days. He wants either a miracle extension of his life, or a death date. Fuck the in-between.

Jarrod extends an arm, his skin the colour of mashed potato, straining, and the blood flushes out of his face as he points out this goof in the DVD extras of *Lord of the Rings*.

I try to have a laugh, agree with the prick, then clear my throat.

"You've been indoors for like a week, man. We should go to Burger Fuel or something, like old times. Get you refreshed before the dinner party tonight."

Jarrod rolls his eyes without looking at me. He's too weak to waste energy turning his head or sitting up. Chemotherapy eats up your insides and leaves you like an empty bag, your muscles melted, your skin burned and bumpy.

"Fine, man. We should at least stretch our muscles. Get the wine glasses and plates from the garage, open some Christmas crackers for the guests. C'mon dude. People wanna say goodbye. You have to, you know… dress the place up a bit. Put up some bunting or whatever."

"The thought is father to the deed," he says. "So go do it."

Jarrod unpauses his Blu-Ray, slips back into his sulk.

We barely speak for the next hour. I remember I haven't raided the bathroom. I go and take his fancy soaps and his razors, hating myself. He tosses his phone at me and I read out the new messages on his Facebook for him, reciting the support and love and prayers while Jarrod snorts and rolls his eyes. He's always taught computing, always loved machines more than people. He's about to leave this world with no missus, no kids. A bit of money from life insurance, a pension from school. Jarrod has three hundred thousand bucks, and all he wants to spend it on is time.

Finally, the credits roll and that's his entire DVD collection over. He's read all his books, watched everything there is to watch. Clocked Skyrim on X-box. Unlocked every easter egg. There's nothing left.

Rain sprinkles the deck. A gust of wind tips a bucket over. His wind chimes tinkle.

"We'll get through this godforsaken dinner party tonight then we'll move on with our lives," Jarrod sighs. "Well, you'll get on with your life. I'll get on with my death."

"Bro –"

"MICHAEL." The sky booms. The roof rattles. "We can slow it down, granted. But we can't stop this thing."

***

At 6.29, just before people file into Jarrod's house for what could be our last dinner party ever, Jarrod and me hover in the coat room while I dust off the bumbag full of drugs me and Jarrod used to take to festivals. There's molly in here, MDMA, enough for a little lick each. The corner of his mouth twitches, almost smiling for the first time in a month. Then he sees Sarmila and Kiran are here and he turns to his audience and hobbles over using his cane.

"Get your photos in," he says, bent, cynical. "This time next month, I'll be worm supper. Hopefully."

Sarmila bursts into tears. Kiran rubs her back and looks at me. I carry on putting out plates and silverware, breadsticks and pate, camembert and olives.

Jarrod was an autistic unsmiling asshole even when he was healthy. He's not going to suddenly become sensitive in his last days.

Jarrod wheels his chair over to the door when the Milners enter, saying "Come in, don't be shy, you know what to do." All the folks here are teachers, mostly. Tall and unimpressed, in thick coats and pointless scarves. Short and nerdy and Euro-politan, in shoes they picked up in Florence or

Buenos Aires. Jarrod plays dictator for the evening, sitting at the head of the table in an office wheely chair with arm rests. He dismisses or hisses or snorts at just about everything anyone says. I watch him while I serve soup and arrange cubes of cheese and pour cocktails. These people have their degrees, Jarrod is thinking, but all they know is life. They know nothing of the undiscovered country Jarrod is about to go to.

I serve roast lamb with mint and rosemary on it, torn off from the untended garden which has been creeping up to the house. After it's been eaten and praised, I slice up a thick chewy moon cake Lisa's mother imported from Taiwan, and Abdi shows off his Chinese. Initially when I check the time, it's 7, and Jarrod's conversation is confrontational, insulting, the guests clamming up, rubbing their wrists, looking at the tines on their forks. Next time I check my watch, it's almost 10 and the windows are black and somebody's just called the deputy principal a cunt and everyone is drunk and leaning back in their chairs, playing with their wine glasses. Someone finds a wrapped box of Cards Against Humanity. By 11.30, Jarrod is slurping whiskey out of the gold-painted plastic cup his students awarded him that day he took them bowling. Usually, Jarrod has three naps a day. Only the molly is keeping him awake right now. I pour wine into Jarrod's gold goblet while his face slumps and collapses on his fist as he rests his flabby melting skull on his knuckles. He's sitting at the head of the table, but there are three conversations going on at once and now it's midnight and the table's a dump of torn garlic bread and glass and salt shakers and bones and corn cobs and quinoa on dirty plates.

We've all had a snort of molly and sucked tequila shots with lemon and salt. The Milners and Ahmed leave together, hugging and kissing Jarrod and taking a farewell selfie with him, kissing Jarrod's bald dome before bursting into tears while Jarrod rolls his eyes.

Next, it's 1 a.m. and even the storm has gone to bed. There's only one conversation going on. Rico is trying to tell us how he's been inspired by this Tibetan monk guy on YouTube who reckons death is nothing to fear. It's like a second life.

"You're giving me advice on death, Rico?"

"Dude, nah, no offence, I just mean, like – Tukdam, Jar. You've never heard of it?"

Jarrod looks at me. My eyebrows narrow.

"I suppose I can tell you a story, this thing I read," Rico is going. He looks over his shoulder warily. His silent sidekick Stacey, or was it Casey, squeezes his arm.

"I don't know if I should. It'll freak you out, Jar."

Jarrod thumps the table. Everybody jumps.

"Do I look like a man with time to waste?"

Rico gets his phone out, clears his throat. "I warned you, okay? This story, it isn't – like, you shouldn't follow it. Don't do what these guys are doing. You're positive you want this story? Came from *Nature*, like the journal *Nature*? Listen. Here we go."

Tukdam, the Tibetan solution to death: science or supposition?

Tukdam appears to be an occurrence in which a Buddhist monk passes away but there is seemingly no physical decomposition for as much as ten to fourteen days. Dr Richard Davidson of Wisconsin Technical College, whose doctoral thesis looked at the meditation's effect on bodily systems, studied the phenomenon at the Deer Park monastery, west of Ann Arbor in December 2019.

The monk Davidson observed, Ongdurje, was aged 84 and suffering from advanced heart disease. Davidson documented the subject tidying his bedroom in the barracks, arranging a disused room, clearing the room's boxes and cobwebs, preparing only a cushion, sitting down and entering a silent, eyes-open transcendental meditation which lasted two hours initially, then stretched out to three, five, and then 24 hours. Silent meditation was all that was required – no chanting; no recital of prayer. The subject simply focuses on walking through the tunnel of death and emerging instead of surrendering, I was told. During this time Ongdurje's pulse slowed to a marginal rate before dropping to zero, though the time of death was impossible to determine. There was no time of death.

Davidson told Nature he wanted to create a model predicting the onset of an "intertidal zone" for subjects whose heart rate slows so much during meditation that it eventually ceases, even while the brain continues to emit gamma waves.

To find out how long life could last after death, Davidson was granted permission to attach electrodes to Ongdurje's temporal and occipital lobes, along with a heart rate monitor, to chart the descent into death – and potentially beyond.

"You walk into the room, what these guys are doing, it's indistinguishable from deep meditation," Davidson said. "Like a deep sleep or a coma. Zero difference. For this guy, for Ongdurje, his chest wasn't even rising and falling. I was there for research interviews; the other monks, they didn't

blink twice about Ongdurje slipping away. They didn't consider Ongdurje to have died, actually; they didn't have a plan to ring a funeral director or anything. While we were waiting to see if, you know, if Ongdurje was going to be – if there were going to be any further developments – they took me to this courtyard, this separate area, in the south wing. This garden full of fuchsias and lilies and vines, kind of neglected. And they were in there. The guys that had done Tukdam before Ongdurje. And at first I thought they were statues. Like cause they were blue statues, the people in the bushes, like Krishna? In Hindu paintings? Cause they'd just… put them there. Left the monks outside in the bushes to sit forever. Exactly like statues. Four of them, I counted, between the bamboo. Sitting cross-legged, lotus-style. So blue that they were black, in the cracks and crevices, like around their armpits and where their heads had sunk into their collars. One guy, I don't know if I should say. It's… like, rats were all over him, yanking at his lips like fish nibbling bait. And he turned – just a smidgen – turned and tilted his head. Nodding. Like saying hello. Real calm. Real beatific.

"That's when I got the hell out of there."

Rico finishes and we all look up.

I yelp. Something is crushing my arm. It's Jarrod, looking more energetic than he has in weeks. Black rings around his eyes.

"You have to get me this Tukdam shit."

Rico has shifted over to the door. He's reaching into the arms of his coat. Stacey-Casey is tightening her scarf and looking anxious. The black world is closing in. It's almost 2, now. The bottom of the night.

Rico hovers, half-turns around. One last look at Jarrod.

"Why would you want to go through

Tukdam? It's not something you can, like, do a weekend retreat on. Forget that Davidson professor guy, anyway. Fucker went crazy, I heard. Made all these weird-ass recordings then *voom*. Up and vanished."

Jarrod flings a glass at Rico. It splinters on the wall. Stacey-Casey ducks, screams, opens the door and escapes.

"GET ME IT." He turns and puts his force on me, eyes narrowing. "Michael, we have to try."

***

Waking Up. That's the name of the app I download. This American-Vietnamese doctor guy, this philosopher, Thich Nhat Hanh, he's the narrator, except he's so robotically calm and quiet and so uninterested in making his English sound normal that you barely recognise it's a guy narrating until you're minutes into it.

Me and Jarrod, we're sitting with our elbows on the kitchen table, hunched over it.

Waking Up Episode 346 is a conversation with that Richard Davidson guy, the doctor, the expert, on the topic of 'second' life. This is what we've been waiting for. Except when Thich Nhat Hanh talks and talks about spiritual planes, and we realise Davidson has hardly said anything, Jarrod goes to the window. It's agonising for him to stand up, and he hobbles, shudders.

"Davidson," Jarrod tells the storm outside. "He's the one we want. He has the answer."

"I already Googled. Plus, I emailed the university. They sacked him, I think, reading between the lines. If he's published something recent, pbbbt…. God knows where. The dude's a ghost, man."

"Even so," Jarrod says, "You need to find him."

***

It's on a Friday after-school drive home to Jarrod's, when the sky is purple, lit by white veins of lightning, and everybody is racing towards their weekend plans, that I decide to try Reddit. Google hasn't helped, nor has LinkedIn or Facebook or the White Pages. But I have a feeling.

I pull over under a service station awning and type Dr Richard Davidson's name into the Reddit app on my phone.

Just a single reference appears in the results. In the single page, a single line.

On a subreddit called r/lifeafterdeath.

A whole discussion board. Someone is getting tons of upvotes. They've pointed to a *Scientific American* article. It says in the natural world, the less something moves, the longer it tends to live. Bacteria thrive on coral for 1000 years in oxygen-low waters. Seeds and spores— practically immortal—can have life spans of thousands of years before rising after a drink of water.

Redditor Friedman69 has an opinion.

You guys read that thing in Nat Geo? CPR = miracle yo. Ask Gardell Thoms, 7 years old. Kid fell in a frozen pond in Amish Country. Didn't breathe for 200 minutes. Pulse returned after they squirted warm fluid up him. You have 2 re-introduce oxygen slowly. I did pre-med at uni. Breathing. That's where we've been going wrong. All this time. Oxygen is a paradox. Take oxygen down to like 0.1 percent, you can keep nematodes alive for a thousand years.

Then there is PneumaTool16.

U guys heard The Blackness Then The White? Audiobook. Banned in 80 countries. U have to get it. Tells u how you can do that Tibetan tukdam thing extend life after death. Last copy of th recording = Pirate Bay but go thru TOR b/c they are watching. It's there. all the instructions. Every other platform dropped the podcast after u-know-what. How the thing took ova him. Shit got real.

I surge out into traffic, push my car through screens of stony rain and race up the motorway.

I burst into Jarrod's home and shake him awake.

"Jar, man. I think I've found it."

***

The garage. That's the place for it, for us. A concrete bunker with a steel door where sceptics and critics can't get in. The place for this whole project to begin. Operation Tukdam.

I push boxes of framed photographs and certificates against the walls. I shove skis and a paddle and hiking boots and 200 sci-fi novels in a wheelbarrow into the corner. I brush the floor clean.

We each position a cushion in the middle of the floor, tighten our wool coats and scarves. I sit easily, though Jarrod packs his painful body down like he's easing into a hot bath, hissing teeth bared.

"You ever meditated before, Jar?"

Jarrod shakes his head. "Pseudo-science, it always seemed to me. Quackery. Hot yoga mumbo-jumbo. Nevertheless: Here we are."

We drum our fingers on our knees. Jarrod is wearing a white t-shirt. His armpits have leaked dark juice into it. Sweat, mixed with something awful and cancerous.

It's raining again today. We can smell it, sneaking through tiny cracks. Relentless drumming on the roof.

I lean forward, position my portable Bluetooth speaker between us. I hold my cellphone in front of me, get ready to push play on a recording that will change Jarrod's life.

Change his death, rather.

For the first time in years, Jarrod looks at me with beseeching eyes.

"Michael. D'you think… d'you think it will, you know… happen immediately?'

"I don't know but, like, you should probably text your dad, eh. Say goodbye."

There is a small window looking out into a chrysanthemum hedge. Jarrod stares at it, then back at the speaker. Jarrod's old man was a lot like him. A robot with as much heart as a calculator. "Just get it over with. Press play."

"Our existence is not a toggle—on for alive, off for dead," begins a slow, plodding, raspy voice. Weary, patient. "Think of our existence as a dimmer switch with which we move through shades white to black."

After a pause, we descend.

"They didn't want me to record this. They wanted me gone. Silenced. But you cannot terminate a dead man.

"This lesson, this sermon, this is my gift to you. You, with multiple sclerosis and 100 pills of paracetamol you're itching to swallow. You, with silicosis and agony in every breath. This, this is for the crippled. The tired. For everyone who has had enough of life."

A pause, then the sickly, crunching sound of a snail being stepped upon.

"If you've ever been diagnosed with squamous cell carcinoma, you'll know the first questions are all variations on why?" continues a voice which bubbles and pops. A sickly voice. Slow and crusted and scabby. A voice trickling with fluid.

"Why are the gods displeased with me?

When did I go wrong? Can't I go back and atone? And your doctor, she's young. Embarrassed. Inexperienced. Turns away on her swivel-chair. Reads the script on her computer screen where there is no emotion.

"*If you've ever been diagnosed with a cancer of the lungs which feels like you have damp sawdust at the bottom of your throat, you'll know every itch, every tired bone, every runny nose precipitates the end.*

"*You'll waste money on therapists and self-help books and inspirational calendars. You'll watch your colleagues hug the wall to avoid brushing against you in the corridors of the faculty office where you once had value. You'll get used to the disappointment of your manager as you take off mornings and afternoons so slim doctors with good skin can pass magnets and radio waves over your body while you lie on a table and imagine what it's like to be a corpse. They'll talk of tomography and you'll know they mean tomb-o-graphy. You'll burst into Deer Park Monastery distraught and drunk with vodka steaming out of your pores at 10 o'clock on a Wednesday night and collapse at the feet of the only people who understand. Tell them you're ready to do this, this tukdam thing. This letting-go. Beg them to let you die here. They'll rub oil into your head, give you a last bath with menthol and incense and the next morning, after a final meal of dhal and rice, they'll guide you to a private room with a cushion in the middle.*"

A pause, now. No breathing. Just that low crunchy slurping like the dregs of a milkshake sucked through a straw. The breath of a man with soggy rotting lungs.

"*In his seminal 1994 text, Erasing Death, critical care physician Sam Parnia reminds us death is a process – not a moment. It's a whole-body stroke. The heart stops beating but the organs don't die immediately. No, organs hang on for quite some time indeed. Organs can be harvested hours after the heart stops.*

"*Consider this, faithful listener: when a liver is rushed across the country to be put in the body of a needier patient, is this not death giving life?*"

I open one eye. I'm surprised to see Jarrod staring directly at me, though he's not looking at me. His chest is barely rising. Jarrod is entranced.

"*You're listening intently, I know. You're getting ready for the second phase. You're looking down a black waterslide.*

Child, this tunnel into which I beckon you. It has an end, you know. You needn't be afraid. At the end is light, refreshing light – a gentle grey light which twists and swirls, like wading through fog. Your eyes will be dry, yes, dry as onion skin. And you will blink in the new world. And you will notice an eyelash twitch and wriggle. You'll pick twisting grains of rice from the rims of your eyes. These things, drinking your juices. They are the children of flies. They are life renewed.

You'll creak and groan as you push yourself to a standing position and wonder what day it is, your hard belly sloshing like a rotten watermelon. How long you've been sitting for. Two weeks, perhaps, or maybe three since you passed over. Feels like an eternity, does it not?

You'll stagger to the door, the hallway, the foyer. The believers, the monks, they'll nod as you pass. As if this were expected. Nothing out of the ordinary. As if you are an equal.

You'll put two hands hard against the very front doors, beside reception and

*the giftshop where postcards and gum
and bonsai trees are sold. You'll notice
something sprouting on your knuckles. The
green mould that grows on bread.*

*Twin boys on tricycles will see you and
drop their ice creams and shriek. The blue
man, mommy, is is is—he's blue—*

*You'll push the glass doors open and here
is the world. You'll put a hand in the centre
of your rib cage. Your heart should be
pounding."*

***

During lunch breaks in the steamy
staffroom, I try to do my research. I try to
listen as Davidson bores through a tunnel
of answers towards the ultimate question. I
keep headphones pressed against my skull
while the teachers chatter and gossip and
spray chewed-up sandwich, elbowing me
to get my input on the new timetable. They
want me to cover a sport for Athletics Day.
They want to know what I think of that
little fuck that got transferred from Marist.
I make my excuses, abandon my box of
papers. I leave a stack of unread memos in
my pigeonhole. This daytime chatter, this
babble and fuss, it's a waste of life. I just
want to be beside my friend as he passes.

It's been eight days of meditation so far. I
don't think he will last until the weekend.

Jarrod has eaten nothing. I've pushed
a sip of water into his lips and not much
else. Any afternoon now, Jarrod is going
to push up from the garage floor and
declare this whole silly experiment a waste
of time. Then he will die and I will shove
his clothes into a giant steel bin beside a
Korean barbecue joint. Place a notice in
the paper. Meet with men in suits.

He appears dead, when I walk in, though
sitting upright. A concrete man, heavy.
Centre of an empty garage. Wind whistling
at the door.

Jarrod's eyes are becoming dry and matte
and I have to brush my palm against his
lashes to make him blink.

In today's sermon, Davidson's plodding
monologue tells of how he had to remain
unresponsive through examinations by
the monks at his monastery while they
murmured and poked and looked at
him hard. They tested for three cardinal
benchmarks. The Tests of Tukdam. The
tests of death.

Davidson describes the tests. I ask Jarrod
if he has a pen and paper somewhere
around here so I can write the instructions
down.

Jarrod says nothing. Jarrod is somewhere
else.

***

In the grey, bruised hour before my
lonely microwave pasta at home, I take my
friend outside and commence the tests of
death. The wind nips, yes. My skin and
Jarrod's is studded with goose pimples,
okay. But the cold will preserve him, I
decided on the drive over, stroking the
shelves at the pharmacy, wondering if I
ought to turn back.

Through the house I drag my friend,
from garage to hallway to the thud-thump-
thud of the steps from the sunken lounge-
pit up to his porch. His ankles scrape the
carpet. His head smacks a corner.

On the wet slippery wooden slats of the
deck, I use scissors to hack off Jarrod's
t-shirt – stiff and brown – and I pull his
right arm until it snaps into place. His
eyelids riffle in the breeze, and a cockroach
runs out of his armpit, but apart from that,
Jarrod doesn't flinch. I find a vein, pull
the pharmacy syringe from my pocket,
unwrap the thing, screw the needle onto

the barrel, shake up a bottle of Betadine and inject 80 millilitres of iodine, then another ten. 90 mils. A huge dose. Jarrod told me to, in the instructions he left me on a Google spreadsheet, before this whole unreal thing became real. Iodine slows oxygen metabolism, he insisted, clutching my collar. My heart needs to sip its oxygen, Michael. To take tiny gasps.

Need to get him cold now. Rip the cotton off his saggy pork-coloured tits. Expose him to the wet wind. Slow down the movement of free radicals and haemoglobin in his cells. I bend him backwards, roll him onto his side, foetal. I take a curtain from the linen closet, spread it over his Pompeii-stiff body, hunched, awkward.

"Jar. JARROD, MAN. You can't hear me. Right?"

The wind answers, speaking through the plastic roof gutters which drizzle a screen of freezing rain. The lawn is soaked, bleeding mud. Brown puddles.

The first test of death is determining whether Jarrod will drink. I cup a handful of rain, pour it in his hard, rubbery purple lips. The water spills out onto his stubbled chin. Jarrod's tongue doesn't move.

Next, I wrench Jarrod's left hand away from his lap. I push back the watch they gave him for 20 years' service at school. I take from my pocket a thin plastic case the size of a business card. A selection of needles I've stolen from the sewing department.

I extract the longest needle, hold it up to the wan light. I mutter sorry for what I'm about to do.

I prise the fingernail back off the skin of the index finger of his left hand (long nail, needs clipping.) I jam the needle into the soft sensitive nailbed, hissing and whimpering on Jarrod's behalf.

Thunder booms like falling logs.

Jarrod doesn't flinch.

Next, I cup another handful of water. I attempt to pour it in his ear. Most of it sits like a pool. A single bubble gurgles to the surface.

And still, Jarrod doesn't move. He is a hunk of defrosting meat.

I set the portable speaker on the deck to continue playing the podcast. I know he's dead, and my eyes are wet, but it feels right. Davidson's voice is Jarrod's guide.

As I walk away, I hear either the wind murmuring under the overhang, or I hear my friend call my name. I don't turn back to check.

I run.

I open my door in a hurry, stagger towards the shower. I warm my skin til the hot water runs out and my teeth have stopped chattering. In bed, I swallow three zopiclone sleeping pills with a slug of schnapps. It's a gift bottle with a note thanking Jarrod for taking the kids to that hackathon in 2014.

I turn the lights out, study the backs of my eyelids.

I wonder what's beyond the blackness.

***

"Jar? You here, bro?"

It's been a week and I've been flopping between druggy daytime sleeps and all-night paranoid Google searches. There are laws requiring you to report a person's death, Reddit tells me. I'm sure I've broken those laws. I've spotted police cars on my drive over here. More cops than normal. They'll be coming for me.

"…broken light grey zone… calling… forest tunnel," says a voice in the house.

Davidson's recording, it has to be. The portable speaker.

"Jarrod? It's me, man. You here?"

I finally locate the voice on the deck. The podcast is still playing. Jarrod's phone has a little life left in it. 24 missed calls.

Richard Davidson's voice is melted and crusty. Exhausted, like a Walkman with dying batteries.

But no Jarrod.

"Dude? You here? I'm sorry about all… I'll call an ambulance or something."

"Kitchen." A voice low and raspy and moist, like a bubble of words burping out of a washbasin.

"DUDE!"

Beside the dishwasher, a single leg sticks out. Suit pants, rumpled as a used condom. A foot. Toes that twitch.

I dip to the lino, crawl to him. He's fallen like a frail old granddad needing a hip replacement. Like a pile of dropped laundry.

Most of a suit is on Jarrod's body. There is a clean white shirt over his distended belly. His arms are inside a black suit jacket. The pants, he must have tried to step into while standing. He's lost his balance and collapsed, unable to bend his stiff body. There is white foam crusted on his lips. His dried-up tempura eyes point in wildly different directions.

"'I'm late," he says, "Have to get to… wurg."

The head speaking to me is lavender. The colour where pink bleeds into purple and cools into blue. Where the skin bunches around his neck, the folds are deep indigo. Blue, too, are the veins snaking across his flesh. Thousands of streams and rivers and tributaries choked with unmoving cold dead blood cells.

"Dude, I don't think you should… School, they're not, like, *expecting* you to work, know what I'm saying? They've pretty much written you off and said goodbye, so the whole suit thing is…"

"They thingb I dead." That mushy throat again. Hard lumpy sticky words. And eyes that roll in their sockets but can't focus. They're cracked eyes, hard and varnished-over, chipped like cue balls dropped on concrete floors. Jarrod is trying to look at me, but something dances on the edge of his vision. As if he can see midges flitting around me.

I pull him to his feet, guide him to the couch.

I put on those Game of Thrones episodes that he loves, Season 4, episodes 1 to 5, specifically, which he's always told me are the height of the show. I position him upright on the couch. As I'm sweeping cobwebs off the ceiling with a broom, I hear his body slide and thud onto the carpet. I drop my broom and rush to help.

He's on his side, after that. Back to the foetal position. No catching up. No reports from beyond. He's a baby again. A pet rock.

But he's still my friend. I can get used to this. We both can.

I will walk with him.

***

A knock at the door wakes me. I've slept in my work shirt and necktie on Jarrod's cold carpet.

It's a real estate woman, carrot-haired, tight belt. Fuckable, gorgeous – but she's trying to peek around the door.

She slides a brochure at me.

Lost a loved one? the brochure says. *It's time to sell.*

I throw the door at her, put my back

against it. Listen as her high heels clack on the path. She's phoning somebody. Some boss or authority or stakeholder. "You guys said he was dead though, right?"

A noise comes from Jarrod. I rush to my friend, check he's okay. It's his stomach. Something is shifting in there.

Later, I insist on getting pizzas delivered. I forbid the Uber Eats guy from coming to the front door, and wait outside on the street for him.

When I drive up and stagger into Jarrod's lounge the next day, exhausted from the all-staff meeting, the pizza appears alive, bubbling and roiling and squirming with black jellybeans. Blowflies. They rise from the pizza, do a dizzying spin, and settle on Jarrod's nose, guzzling the stream of brain fluid that flows through his nostrils and pools above his lips.

The pizza is not the meal. The meal is my friend.

I try to bathe him, on the fourth day. To get him to move, I have to stand under him, and juices and scabs stain my tie and shirt. I tip Jarrod into the tub, pull his underwear off. Maggots around his cock. I begin with a blast of warm water until Jarrod's purple hand reaches out and squeezes mine.

"No," he gasps. Melting, rotting, weary voice. "*Cold.*"

***

Jarrod—the new Jarrod, the changed Jarrod, the passed-over Jarrod—cannot comprehend time. I put on another of his favourite films, *Dune*, and after hours have passed and the credits have run til the end, he remains staring at a black screen. The flies return, big shiny jellybean-sized bluebottles, drinking his eyes while he gawps. Later, when I haul him off the

couch and we stagger to the bedroom, I observe a pool of maggots in his wake, wriggling yellow grains of rice that fall around his ankles. I clean his socks in the sink, though the smell is impossible to conquer. The salty stench of rotting shoes pulled from a muddy river.

Mornings, I sit him on a backyard bench to watch birds. I give him a log of luncheon meat. He chews, pulls the soft pink meat into his decaying throat. I hear the meat roil and churn in his belly, which has become a swollen hump, pushing out against the depressing wool jersey I've forced on him. On a Thursday, I race to his place from work and walk in and have to stride to the kitchen to turn a tap off. An inch of water has pooled in the kitchen, the larder and laundry. He's been leaving lights on, too, as he lurches up and down his house, haunting rooms, leaning against walls for hours, leaving sticky smears on the wallpaper where juices leak through his back, soaking the pathetic suit jacket he wears for a job he'll never attend.

Then the electric company shuts the power off. No more lights or warm water. No more DVD marathons.

***

After ten days, we walk to the park, me with a hand around his crumbling shoulders, urging him like an old man. Spring is coming down. The wind nibbles with gums instead of teeth.

On a bench looking through the roundabout and bark chips and rope cage, we gaze toward the brook. A girl comes up the grass slope, clutching a fistful of broken-off bulrushes, babbling *Hotdogs, hotdogs, getcha hotdogs.*

Her eyes lock with Jarrod's. She trembles, begins rocking side to side. The girl's pants are yellow at first. As she takes in the horror on the bench beside me, her pants turn black.

The pier, the week after. Slapping wind, blades of sun. Wet droplets in the air. Seagulls circling.

"Bad here," Jarrod is mumbling, "See them waiting. End of the pier. Mouths. Tails."

Jarrod more inflexible, harder to lug and heft, his legs stiff as glass.

"What's waiting?"

"Them. Swarm. People… black. Devils. Want me. To join… legion."

Jarrod's foot comes down in a crack. He twists. I hear his tibia snap. He bends, wobbles. Falls over on his back, his foot upside down, twisted as a fettucine noodle. Seagulls immediately bomb us, nipping, tearing, squawking. They land and begin gobbling mouthfuls of meat from Jarrod's snapped-off foot, a white bone oozing brown blood in a leg that's blue.

As we run toward the car, a rottweiler wrestles out of the leash-grip of a woman on rollerblades and bounds after Jarrod. I manage to get the car door open and Jarrod secured just as the dog bumps the side, arfing.

I drive us home. There is a long sleek brick of a car in the driveway. A black hearse.

Behind it, an ambulance, and a skinny police officer, all uniform, neat shaven head, blue hat, notepad. I keep the car running, idle past, sure I can see in the rearview the funeral director step out onto the street with a paramedic beside him, pointing as I disappear.

I'm in trouble. But I want to protect my friend.

***

X-Base Backpackers on Queen Street. A place we last came to when we were 19 and ridiculous. We take a dorm room. Downstairs, breaking glass and shouting. French girls chanting. Relentless nightclub *unst-unst-unst.*

"It's over, Jar," I say, sniffing the disgusting hostel pillow. "We gotta face it, dude. If there was a way out, a shaft of light or something, you'd've said so, right?"

I'm pacing wall to wall, peeling awful green leaf-patterned wallpaper, dark and hopeless and depressing. I pace because I think I can walk out of all this. Walk til they forget, at school, that I abandoned the job. Walk til the police and health services and coroner forget that a man died at 2289 Mairangi Drive and his body disappeared, parts of a foot later discovered at Murray's Bay Wharf. I pace and peel wallpaper and Jarrod lies a metre away on a tomb-sized bunk, two arms and 1.5 legs, as if practising for his coffin.

His stomach is slopping and rippling like he's got hunger cramps, so I sneak him down the Fire Stairs and drive us to Burger Fuel. Our old favourite. Our routine.

I pull up in a disabled parking space, right outside the restaurant, where tarmac meets concrete gutter meets linoleum.

It reeks in the car. I open a window.

"Hungry," Jarrod gasps, drunk with death, hair trickling down his skull, head lolling and wobbling. "Hung – hunger – you've… you have to– "

A river of yellow fluid blurghs from his mouth, sickly thick custard. As he's beginning to say sorry, fumbling to open the car door, a second torrent of maggots pours onto my lap. He's vomiting so hard he's pushed back. He squeezes the door open. Jarrod, puffy and blue, falls out onto the tarmac, begins to move, toward Burger Fuel, away from Burger Fuel. Anywhere. But he cannot walk with just one foot. He can't even get on his feet. Instead, tearing his knees open, he crawls.

A family tips over their table and runs as the blue lumpy creature in a torn black suit reaches out, begging for a helping hand to pull him up. Panic. Spilled chips. Overturned burgers. Screams and roars and me, cursing Jarrod as I wrap my arms around him and haul 80 kilograms of meat toward the tarpaulin-lined trunk of the car that's just big enough to fit a man, except his head is sticking out. Hanging over the licence plate and the towbar. I can't cram the corpse any further into the boot and the Burger Fuel manager has a phone against his ear and he's slipping on squashed chips, asking police to come immediately, and I have to get the trunk closed so I slam it right on his neck and blurt SORRY, JAR, OHMYGOD I'M SO SO SO SORRY and I crouch and catch the blue squishy coconut as the last flap of neck-skin detaches and it falls to the tarmac.

Catch my friend.

Catch his head.

***

South of Auckland is Pukekohe. South of Pukekohe, the expressway lets us drive at 120 kays an hour. South of that, back-roads through Limestone Downs. Green wilderness. All valleys and castle of rock. Hedges and fields of waving corn. There are surprises over each hill and corner, and eventually, warm signs counting the kilometres, then Te Awamutu, and Smith Street, where I ease back the throttle as the orange empty light comes on.

I phoned him last night. While Jarrod slept. Had a talk on Skype, actually. Richard Davidson wouldn't say which country he was in, but I've got a theory. I think it's Bhutan. I think he's high up in mountains where the air is cool. In the snow, maybe. Refrigeration.

Davidson – who took a hundred emails and seven phone calls and a ton of private Reddit messages to track down – contains himself in a hoodie and says nothing. His face is darkened. I'm not even sure if there is a human in there. I can tell he's in a tent, talking to me. He listens as I tell my story. We've been winning, I argue, we did okay. We got through. But there's not much left of my friend. And I don't know where we're going.

The man in the tightly-drawn hoodie says little. It is only when the sleeping bag he's rested his laptop on shifts and catches fresh light that I see a snapshot. That skull, from the Misfits logo. A skull with eyeballs in it shrunken like marbles. That's what's inside the hoodie. A skull without eyebrows or sideburns or nostrils or lips. All bone and eyeballs.

Finally, a noise comes out of him.

"Wish I had a fren," the skull says, "Fren like you."

A bone falls out from under his teeth. He is fumbling for it, pressing his detaching jaw back into his throat when he terminates the call.

***

The woman behind the reception counter looks like she's been tumbled under a truck. Violently bleached hair with black roots. Engine grease on her fingers. Rubbing a keycard against her hip, suspicious.

"You ain't got much luggage."

We're at the Pirongia View Motel. Two

stars. Hardly an establishment to fight over. I tell her I just need a room. Farthest from the road. No windows, I don't care. We just need shelter. And she has to let me know if any cops come past.

"You can wash that, you know, your towel," she says, leading us across the gravel. "We got a laundry. What you got in there, anyway – a bowling ball? Me, I love to bowl."

"Totally," I say, shifting the big round weight from the crook of my right arm to my left. "Bowling, right."

The windowless motel cube we hole up in feels safe. It's our bunker, our fortress. There is unlimited SkyTV. A block of showers and sinks. Fish and chips over the road, not that Jarrod will eat anything.

After dinner, we kick back on the bed and watch *South Park* and I guffaw til I cry.

Jarrod's eyelids are half-down. He looks sleepy.

This laundry that the hag at Reception mentioned, I'll be needing it. I'm almost ready to think of tomorrow. Depends if tomorrow comes or not. Because if I do wake tomorrow, I'll need to do intense, heavy, hot washing. The bowling ball bag is so saturated with juices that it drips. And I'll need to get the bloodstains out of the bed before the motel asks questions. He's leaking, Jarrod is. Soaking through the sheets. His cut-off neck oozes endless fluid, much of it blackish-brown blood. Other fluid is clear stuff with pink veins in it, like crab guts, that cascades out of his nostrils like a sticky moustache, pooling on lips that he struggles to lick. It's the frontal cortex of his brain, putrefying.

We watch silly shows til midnight and I even pop out for a bottle of wine and come back and ransack the cupboards and find

a plastic sippy cup. I pour wine into my friend's lips and it gushes through his jaw, fingers of wine and brainjuice trickling across the bedspread, but it's okay. I believe Jarrod appreciates the gesture. His eyes have shrivelled to nearly nothing, now. Switched off, with just a little afterglow.

Me, I turn the motel lights out and crawl under the wet covers, wriggling til I find a dry spot. I roll on my side and stroke my friend's scalp. I have to halt the stroking every 30 seconds, wipe off chunks of skin and sticky hair.

In the blue hour before dawn, we listen to trucks rumble past. Hear a fight, broken glass somewhere. A cat's claws on a steel drum.

"Goodnight, Jar. Love you, bro."

In the blackness, I see two teeth appear as his lips pull back and his cheeks fold.

A smile.

ANIMAL PARADE
BY DANI RINGROSE
WINNER OF THE 2021 ROBERT N STEPHENSON
FLASH FICTION COMPETITION

The dust that had covered the horizon for weeks now was grubby white, like someone had taken an eraser to the bottom half of the sky. I looked out the window of my vet surgery to see whether the sky had shifted in the frenzied hours I'd spent here. There was no fire here. Yet. The dust, acrid and sharp, trespassed in my sleep and tasted metallic, like blood. The little sleep I had over the last fortnight was sporadic and nibbled at between jobs.

Everything was on fire; we were going to lose it all. More than just the vet surgery, or my job. The bushfires might navigate their way here and destroy my business, but it was the insidious, prickly fingers of fire that would touch the whole country I was more worried about.

Animals piled up on our porch outside, a backlog so big at one point it looked like a toddler's pile of plush toys –if the toddler had taken to their toys with a match, or charcoal paints, or pulled a button off a face.

For each day as humans have moved forward, our actions—or inaction—was wiping out a new animal every day. A wren here, another wallaby there. *They all look the same, they said; we only need to keep one type of wallaby, the rest of the world can't tell the difference.*

In front of me, splayed on the surgical table, was the last Brush-Tailed Rock Wallaby. I knew its appearance easily; in the wild its tail already appeared singed. Its eyes were coal, but lacked the life that would normally bounce around in them. I was racing against time to try and restore their spark. Vulcanisation had long gone out of fashion, but here I was, transgressing against all reasonable advice from my peers, ready to zap the last Australian land animals back to life.

Alone in the surgery, I stayed up too late last night, and rather than logging my progress, I had fallen asleep, slumped against my keyboard. In my dreams, the rock wallaby was upright, facing me; it turned, and revealed with one paw the procession of broken and damaged extinctions that stretched long behind it, longer than any wallaby tail.

The koala, carried triumphantly by the last bulldozer that felled its home. Carpet pythons, swelled in the throat by the poisoned possums they had tried to swallow. Thylacenes strutted behind bars. Cassowaries, their proud dinosaur heads bowed. Snuffling echnidas, shuffling towards their snuffing-out.

On and on, the brolga luridly dancing over the parade of bodies.

A cawing woke me; three crows perched on my window like the witches from Macbeth. Already surrounded by corpses, the covids' role as harbinger of death had been stripped from them. More mobile and agile, these birds will live, the black feathers will not show damage, the scavengers will move on. Listlessly, I waved my hand at them and growled *shoo*, the noise caught in the grey, gravelly ash stuck in my throat.

I moved back to the surgical table, and switched my systems back on. Under usual circumstances, the flickering of lights that occurred simultaneously would've made me uneasy, but I was mining the power, the heart, of electricity, for life. Coal-fired, that which had fuelled the increase in temperatures, and bushfires, would also bring what it had wiped out back to life. Was I just delaying the inevitable, expanding the circle of death? Where what kills and subsequently brings things back to life will eventually kill them again.

As I'd strapped the pads to the wallaby's limbs, kookaburras cackled in the distance.

My husband should've been here to help me, but I'm not sure he would've approved. He was a dabbler of all trades. He was a vet like myself, yes, a co-owner of this surgery we established in a clearing on the edge of a small town neither of us had heard of until we pointed our finger at a map. But he was also our electrician, our mechanic, our builder. Yet he was currently none of these; he was in the thick of the dust, the smoke, fighting the fires that threatened our adopted town.

And I was alone, surrounded by sharp fluorescent surgical lights, the musk and decay of dead fur, and a tangy wind that brought the ever-present threat of fire.

My sleep had put me behind schedule: if I couldn't save this wallaby, perhaps it was the koala slumped on the lino beside the surgical trolley I could rescue. A bottle of antiseptic was sharp enough to snap me back to attention. I rubbed its limbs hastily with the liquid, for no reason beyond habit. Attaching a fresh set of pads to its limbs, I flicked knobs on the control panel.

It had, at one point in its evolution, been a machine to stimulate muscle in elderly patients at a respite centre. After my father had passed away, I had removed it from his empty shell of a room.

The machine crackled, like the static on our two-way radio. Wallaby fur bristled, and matched the hair on the back of my hands. With a twist, it hummed with life, and for one brief moment, the black tail snapped against my arm. Encouraged, I wrenched the power even higher. A sharp pain fizzed through my palms, and found its way to my skull.

This time, the dreams were deeper, and full of sound. Dingoes howled for their lost packs, their voices bouncing back unanswered. In the distance, the reaches of time, the ancients marched towards me, desperate to be a part of my wild experiment. A giant wombat wombled expectantly. A cluster of thunderbirds rampaged down the procession of extinction.

And the serpent of creation, its jaws open wide, curved around in an ouroboros, turned its eye to me. Its tongue flickering with electricity.

GUEST EDITOR

GREG CHAPMAN is a two-time Bram Stoker Award® and multiple Australian Shadows Award-nominated author, illustrator and book cover designer, based in Brisbane. He is the author of several novels, novellas and short story collections, including, *Hollow House*, *The Noctuary: Pandemonium* and *Netherkind*, *The Last Night of Octobe*r, *This Sublime Darkness and Other Stories* and *Bleak Precision*. The first graphic novel he illustrated, *Witch Hunts: A Graphic History of the Burning Times*, (McFarland & Company) written by authors Rocky Wood and Lisa Morton, won the Superior Achievement in a Graphic Novel category at the Bram Stoker Awards® in 2013. Greg was also the President of the Australasian Horror Writers Association from 2017-2020. His websites are darkscrybe.com and dark-designs.com

CONTRIBUTOR BIOGRAPHIES

J. ASHLEY-SMITH is a British–Australian author of dark speculative fiction and co-host of the Let The Cat In podcast. J's stories have been shortlisted for multiple awards, winning both the Australian Shadows Award and Aurealis Award. His first book, *The Attic Tragedy*, won the Shirley Jackson Award. His short story collection, *The Measure of Sorrow*, is due for release in 2023 from Meerkat Press. J. gathers moth dust in the suburbs of North Canberra, tormented by the desolation of telegraph wires.

GERALDINE BORELLA writes fiction for children, young adults and adults. Her stories and poems have been published by Deadset Press, IFWG Publishing, Busybird Publishing, Celapene Press, Wombat Books/Rhiza Edge, AHWA/Midnight Echo, Antipodean SF, Black Ink Fiction, Shacklebound Books and Raven and Drake Books. She enjoys the exploratory nature of speculative fiction, writing across sub genres. She lives in Far North Queensland, Australia, on Njadon-Jii land and is currently working on several longer writing projects, inbetween writing for short story call outs. You can find more about her at https://geraldineborella.com/about/ , https://www.facebook.com/geraldineb4/ and at https://mobile.twitter.com/geraldineborel2

New Zealander **MICHAEL BOTUR** (born 1984) is the author of 12 books including *The Lockdownland Trilogy*, a young adult dystopian novel series (publisher Next Chapter, 2022) and the breakthrough novel *Crimechurch*. He has won awards for short fiction writing in three countries and has published journalism in most major NZ newspapers and magazines. Botur led the ground-breaking #100NZStories100Days campaign in 2019. He lives in Northland with two talented children who starred in the book, *My Animal Family*. In 2021, Botur won the Australasian Horror Writers Association's Robert N Stephenson Short Story Competition for Test of Death (which features in this issue).

KAT CLAY is a writer, critic, and content producer from Melbourne. Her short story 'Lady Loveday Investigates' won three prizes at the 2018 Scarlet Stiletto Awards, including the Kerry Greenwood Prize for Best Malice Domestic. Kat's short stories have been published in *Interzone, Cosmic Horror Monthly, Aurealis*, and several anthologies. Her non-fiction and criticism has been published in The Guardian, The Victorian Writer, and Weird Fiction Review, and she was a contributor to the Locus winning and Hugo nominated *Dangerous Visions and New Worlds: Radical Science Fiction*, 1950 to 1985.

MATTHEW R. DAVIS is an award-winning author and musician based in Adelaide, South Australia. He's been shortlisted for a Shirley Jackson Award, a WSFA Small Press Award, and multiple Australian Shadows and Aurealis Awards, winning two Shadows in 2019—his previous publication in Midnight Echo, "This Impossible Gift", was shortlisted for a Shadows Award in 2017. He's published around seventy short stories and his books include *If Only Tonight We Could Sleep* (collection, Things in the Well, 2020), *Midnight in the Chapel of Love* (novel, JournalStone, 2021), and *The Dark Matter of Natasha* (novella, Grey Matter Press, 2022), with more on the way soon. He's the bassist/vocalist in heavy bands such as Blood Red Renaissance and icecocoon when they're active, and he likes to explore abandoned buildings and other creative avenues with his photographer partner Meg. Find out more at matthewrdavisfiction.wordpress.com.

DR STEPHEN DEDMAN is the author of *The Art of Arrow Cutting, Shadows Bite, Immunity*, two *Shadowrun* tie-in novels, the non-fiction book *May the Armed Forces Be With You: The Relationship Between Science Fiction and the United States Military*, and more than 120 short stories published and reprinted in an eclectic variety of anthologies and magazines. He's reviewed books for *The West Australian, Australian Book Review* and *Science Fiction*, and taught creative writing at UWA and the Forensic Science Centre. He's worked as a bookseller, game designer, editor, actor, museum exhibit and experimental subject, and was an associate editor of *Eidolon* and fiction editor of *Borderlands*. He's won Aurealis and Ditmar awards, and been nominated for the Bram Stoker Award, the BSFA Award, the Sidewise Award, the Seiun Award, the Spectrum Award, and a sainthood. For a list of his work, go to www.stephendedman.com

CLAIRE FITZPATRICK is an award-winning author of speculative fiction, non-fiction, and poetry. She is the 2020 recipient of the Rocky Wood Memorial scholarship fund for her non-fiction anthology '*A Vindication Of Monsters—Essays on Mary Shelley and Mary Wollstonecraft*' (soon to be published by IFWG Publishing) and the winner of the 2017 Rocky Wood Award for Non-Fiction and Criticism for 'The Body Horror Book'. Her 2019 debut collection *Metamorphosis* was received with praise. She has been a panellist at various conventions and is currently working on her dark fantasy novel. She'll finish it. One day. Visit her at www.clairefitzpatrick.com.au

REBECCA FRASER is a Melbourne-based author of genre-mashing fiction for children and adults, with a penchant for the weird and unsettling. Her work has won, been shortlisted for, and honourably mentioned for numerous awards and prizes. Rebecca's publications include over sixty short stories, poems, and articles in Australian and international anthologies, journals, and magazines. Her longer works include three middle grade novels, and a collection of short dark fiction. The first in her forthcoming fantasy trilogy *Jonty's Unicorn* (Book 1 of The Irrawene Chronicles) will be released in 2023 (IFWG Publishing Australia). Say G'day at www.rebeccafraser.com or Twitter/Insta @becksmuse

MICHAEL HUGHES lives in Melbourne with his partner, son, two dogs, and possessed cat. Growing up in rural Tasmania, he was introduced to the works of authors such as Stephen King, Richard Laymon and H.P. Lovecraft at a young age, who filled him with a creeping dread that he has carried with him ever since. He has a love of everything horror and wants nothing more than for his stories to keep you up wondering at night.

PAMELA JEFFS lives in Queensland, Australia. Daughter to a Greek immigrant mother and an Australian father she is proud of her mixed heritage. Pamela has published four short story collections, co-authored '*The Zookeeper's Tales of Interstellar Oddities*' with Aiki Flinthart and has 70+ short stories featured in various other publications including '*Relics, Wrecks and Ruins*', by CAT Press and '*Andromeda Spaceways Inflight Magazine*'. She has been shortlisted for multiple awards, including numerous Aurealis Awards, a Ditmar Award and she has been twice noted in the Writers of the Future Competition. For more information, visit her at www.pamelajeffs.com or on Facebook @ pamelajeffsauthor.

CHRIS MASON is an award-winning author who lives on Peramangk land in the Adelaide Hills of South Australia. Her stories have appeared in numerous publications, including the Things in the Well anthologies, and the Australasian Horror Writers Association's magazine *Midnight Echo*. Chris has won Aurealis Awards for Best Horror Short Story and Best Horror Novella, received the Australian Shadows Paul Haines Award for long fiction, and been shortlisted for a Shirley Jackson Award. You can visit Chris at: facebook.com/chrismasonhorrorwriter or on twitter @Chris_A_Mason.

DANI RINGROSE is an emerging Australian gothic author who lives in Brisbane. She is a high school literature teacher, where she gets to indulge in her love of creative writing with the most amazing students. She loves the terrifying opportunities the Australian landscape and its history has to offer the world of horror, and is inspired by the 100 acres of bushland she owns in the Scenic Rim with her husband and mum.

D.I. RUSSELL is a British-Australian horror author who lives in Western Australia. He is author of the *Horrificata* series (for teen readers), *Samhane, Scream Ride, Playthings*, the *Mind Terrors* novellas, *Mother's Boys, Tricks, Mischief and Mayhem*, and *Entertaining Demons*.

SHANE K. RYAN has been creating horror art for most of his life. Starting off as a traditional artist creating macabre and surreal drawings which have been featured by the likes of Fangoria and Gore Master. He has won open fantasy art competition awards and had his work displayed in several international art exhibitions. He then moved into digital art where he has worked on posters for various independent horror films and created cover art for music artists, such as the pioneer of horror-core rapper Ganksta N-I-P. He is now working in the 3D-art space for various major horror publishers.

DEBORAH SHELDON is an award-winning author from Melbourne, Australia. She writes across the darker spectrum of horror, crime and noir. Latest titles include *The Again-Walkers, Liminal Spaces: Horror Stories*, and *Man-Beast*. Award-nominated titles include *Body Farm Z, Contrition, Devil Dragon, Thylacines*, and *Figments and Fragments: Dark Stories*. Her collection *Perfect Little Stitches and Other Stories* won the Australian Shadows 'Best Collected Work' Award. She has won the Australian Shadows 'Best Edited Work' Award twice: for *Midnight Echo 14* and *Spawn*. Her short fiction has appeared in respected magazines and 'best of' anthologies, and received various award nominations. Other credits include TV scripts, feature articles, non-fiction books and award-winning medical writing. Visit Deb at http://deborahsheldon.wordpress.com

MARK TOWSE would sell his soul to the devil or anyone buying if it meant he could write full-time. Alas, he left it very late to begin this journey, penning his first story since primary school at the ripe old age of 45. Since then, he's published in many anthologies and journals and had his work produced on countless podcasts. His most recent novella, *One Last Shindig* from D&T Publishing, was published in March 2022.

www.ingramcontent.com/pod-product-compliance
Lightning Source LLC
Chambersburg PA
CBHW081919130726
47909CB00015B/3035